The Topsy-Turvy Kingdom

More Stories for Your Faith Journey

James L. Henderschedt

RESOURCE PUBLICATIONS, INC.
San Jose, California

Editorial director: Kenneth Guentert
Production editor: Kathi Drolet
Page layout and production: Elizabeth J. Asborno
Cover production: Terri Ysseldyke-All

Reprint Department
Resource Publications, Inc.
160 E. Virginia Street, #290
San Jose, CA 95112-5848

Library of Congress Cataloging in Publication Data

Henderschedt, James L., 1936-
   The Topsy-Turvy Kingdom: More Stories for Your Faith Journey
/James L. Henderschedt.
       p.   cm.
   ISBN 0-89390-177-6
   1. Christian fiction, American.   I. Title.
   PS3558.E4797T6   1990
   813'.54—dc20
                                        89-49291
                                        CIP

5 4 3 2 1 | 94 93 92 91 90

Some of these stories originally appeared in Celebration *magazine.*

These stories are dedicated to all pilgrims on a faith journey who pause to rest along the way at hostels where the telling or reading of stories gives nourishment and strength for the adventure. Especially do I dedicate them to the troubadour who has been my story-telling companion as I make my way toward the Kingdom: Father Ed Hays.

Contents

Introduction

Stories always have been, and continue to be, important for communicating and understanding the
Gospel message of salvation through God's Son,
Jesus Christ. Stories are the way familiar truths are
passed on from generation to generation. They verbalize
the witness of someone who has found his or her joy and
peace in that Redeemer.

Recently I experienced how true this is. A discussion in
an adult Christian education class addressed the personal
meaning of the Sacrament of the Altar. People began telling stories. They were not usually free to openly express
themselves. But one after the other, they shared brief
pericopes out of their lives and told how God's gift
through the simple meal led them out of the depths of
despair, away from destructive thoughts, above crippling
and debilitating emotions. In the Sacrament, God was at
work in their lives; in their stories, God was at work
crafting the witness of the presence of his Kingdom in
our midst.

Through the medium of storytelling, people can address
issues normally too painful or sensitive to discuss openly.
Hidden beneath real or fictional people, contained in

events experienced or created, are the joys and sorrows, the successes and failures, the hopes and despairs of the storyteller and the hearer. Through related discoveries and struggles, your story becomes my story, and my story strikes responsive cords in your memories.

Often stories are not complete. Other times we may not be absolutely sure of their meaning. This can be frustrating to people who need things neat and conveniently packaged. But, for the one who is truly in search of the Kingdom in our midst, the unfinished story affords the opportunity to be a part of the resolution, and the mysterious meaning demands pondering and mystical meditation.

Once again, this collection of stories grew out of my never-ending journey. At times they draw me closer to a realization of what it means to be a child of God; at other times I am left to ponder an unsolvable mystery. A few have been previously published in *Celebration,* and I have received correspondence from pastors, priests, and laity who have expressed their appreciation for being able to reflect on the stories and use them for their own spiritual adventure. I welcome you to the journey for which these stories may serve as a map, whether you are struggling in the aloneness of your personal meditation or in the fellowship of others who are seeking their spiritual maturity.

Above all, I pray that this book will give you the key to unlock the treasury in which the wealth of your stories are contained. I pray that you will join the growing ranks of people who, sharing the Good News of life and salvation in Jesus Christ, will gather together all who will listen with eager ears, and tell your story.

The Wooden Crate

Theme: armor of God
Scripture: Ephesians 6:10-18
Season: general Pentecost theme

Peg and Ted Watson sat cross-legged on the floor of their living room, staring at the wooden crate between them. Peg had a worried look on her face as she contemplated its size. Ted's face showed intrigue because of the strange sound it had made when it was crudely dropped by the person making the delivery. Both of them wondered what was in the box; however, they would not be able to find out until their son, Paul, returned from school because this, like so many that had come before, was addressed to Paul, and every one was sent by Ted's brother, Dave.

"Oh, Ted," Peg worried, "I wonder what Dave sent Paul now?"

Ted shook his head. "I surely don't know. I wouldn't even be able to make a guess. All of the gifts he has sent Paul have been so..." he hesitated, "strange."

Peg responded with an involuntary shiver. "Paul's room is beginning to look like a museum of natural history. I really think it is nearly out of hand. It's actually spooky in there. I don't know how Paul can even sleep. The walls have those grotesque ceremonial masks from Africa; there are those strange rocks from Central America, and that huge tiki carving from New Zealand. But what I really can't stand is that stuffed cobra and mongoose from India. I keep thinking that they are not dead." Peg responded with another shiver.

Ted chuckled. "I guess we have to pay the price of my having a younger brother who is a world traveler with strange interests. His heart is in the right place, though," he continued. "He certainly loves Paul. I have never seen anyone prouder to be a sponsor at a baptism as Dave was when Paul was baptized. I really think he is doing this because he has a need to fulfill his responsibilities."

"Maybe so, but—" Peg's answer was interrupted by the sound of the front door opening. Paul was home from school. "Mom, Dad," Paul called out as he did every day.

"In here, sport," Ted called.

Paul came to the doorway, his arms were filled with books and papers. "Hi," he said. Then he saw the wooden crate. "Wow!" he exclaimed. "What's that?"

"We don't know," Peg answered. "We were waiting for you to come home."

"Is that for me?" Paul asked excitedly. "Is it from Uncle Dave?"

"You got it," answered his father. "I have the tools right here. If you want to, we can start to open it now."

Paul could hardly contain himself. "Yes, let's open it now."

Ted reached behind him and came up with a crow bar and hammer. Slowly and carefully, he and Paul started to pry the top off the wooden crate. After a while the lid came off and Peg, Ted, and Paul stared at the contents of the crate.

"Oh boy!" Paul shouted.

"Oh my," said Ted.

"Oh no," fretted Peg.

"It's a suit of armor," exclaimed Paul. "Let's take it out of the box."

Piece by piece, the strange gift was taken from the crate. It was old and marked from many battles. The helmet was dented in a number of places. The leather breastplate with brass ornaments bore scars that spoke of numerous close encounters with death. The shield was battered; the sword was nicked; the special sandals were severely worn.

Ted noticed some strange markings on each of the pieces, but he could not make out what they were. Paul saw them too. He was holding the helmet when a folded piece of paper fell from inside. Paul picked it up and unfolded it. He gave it to his father, who said, "It is a letter to you from your Uncle Dave. Shall I read it to you?"

"Yes, please," Paul said to his father. "Please read it to me."

Paul put the helmet on his head. It was much too big for him, but as far as he was concerned, it fit perfectly. He sat down on the floor next to his father and listened as the letter was read.

Dear Paul,

By now your father is probably bewildered and your mother is worrying about where she is going to put my latest gift. I found it in a market here in Istanbul, and as soon as I saw it I knew it had to be for you. I know it is pretty big for you now, but I am sure that some day you will grow into it.

I had to buy it for you when I saw it. It is special armor, Paul, and I not only want you to have it, but I want you to understand what it means. Just a few years ago, I was the sponsor at your baptism. I promised to help your mother and father to be an example and to help you understand what it means to be loved by God through Jesus.

That is not an easy task, and being a Christian can be very difficult in today's world. I think the man who once owned this armor understood. You will notice some markings on each of the pieces of armor. They are Greek words that were scratched in. This is what the words mean:

On the helmet is the word for "salvation."

The belt buckle has the word "truth" inscribed on it.

On the shield you will find in large letters, "faith."

The breastplate bears the marks for "righteousness."

The sandals interestingly are marked with the words, "the Gospel of peace."

Finally, if you draw the sword out of the scabbard, you will see that this soldier etched on the words, "Word of God."

You see, Paul, these are the things we want you to have. They are the gifts of your baptism, and they are those things that will help to win the battle against anything or anyone who would try to take you away from God. It is not the weapon or the armor itself, but what they represent. With truth, faith, the Gospel of Peace, and the Word of God, salvation and righteousness will be yours. The saint after whom you were named once said, "Put on the whole armor of God."

I pray that God's armor will protect you. And please tell your mother and father that I just can't help myself. Especially, assure your mother that the cobra and mongoose are dead.

Uncle Dave

Ted, Peg, and Paul sat in silence, looking at the pile of old, worn, rusting armor. Each one was thinking of the soldier who once went to battle with the words of St. Paul etched on it. Ted finally broke the silence. "Well, sport, " he said, "your Uncle Dave sure knows how to take care of his buddy, doesn't he?"

Paul smiled at his father. "He sure does. With what he gave me, not even old Satan will be able to stand up against me."

Peg whispered a prayer that only she and he Lord heard, "And I pray that he won't have to use it too often. Be with him, Lord, so that he can withstand the forces that would take him away from you."

Ted and Peg started to pick up the pieces of armor that were strewn over the living room floor. Now came the task of finding a place for it. Paul stood, oversized helmet coming down over his eyes and ears. In one hand he held the shield of faith and in the other the sword of God's Word. He was truly a baptized soldier of Christ.

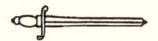

Lord God, the battle goes on. The enemy would seek to capture me and take me away from your presence. I cannot fight the battle by myself. But, with the armor you provide—the belt of truth, the breastplate of righteousness, the sandals of the Gospel of Peace, the shield of faith, the helmet of salvation, the sword of the Spirit that is the Word of God—I will be able to fight the good fight. Be by my side, my strength and guide, and lead me always on the path of faithfulness. Amen.

Jon's Wild Ride

Theme: hope in a hopeless world
Scripture: Hebrews 11:1
Season: 12th Sunday in Pentecost (Cycle C)

The Olson family had saved a long time to take this vacation. Ever since the Fabulous World of Fantasy had opened, the children had wanted to go. But Texas was so far, and everything was so expensive. At best, Jon, Ina, and their three children, Ingrid, Al, and Inez, could dream about the time when they would be able to fulfill their dream.

Everyone knows that in order for dreams to come true the dreams need a little help from the dreamers. So the Olson family made an agreement with each other that, every chance they had, they would save some money and put it aside for their vacation at the Fabulous World of Fantasy.

In order to do this, they all had to agree to do without some of the things they wanted. It wasn't long before everyone realized how difficult this was going to be. Jon had to sacrifice a new table saw for his workshop; Ina had to have her aging dishwasher repaired instead of replaced; Ingrid had to give up the idea of having a compact disc player; Al had to wear no-name sneakers; and Inez had to be satisfied with hand-me-downs. It was a long, hard road.

But they finally made it. There was enough money in the bank for the trip to the Fabulous World of Fantasy. If asked, they would still admit that it was something that they could not afford to do. However, with the children getting older, they also new that they could not afford to put it off any longer.

The drive was long, tiresome, and endless. As each mile passed, the excitement in the Olson's automobile mounted. None of the children asked, "Are we almost there?" though they wanted to just about every ten minutes. It took three days of driving, staying at budget motels, eating sandwiches that they had packed, and frequent fuel and potty stops, but they made it. A cheer went up when Ina read, "Welcome to Waco."

That night was a restless night in the Olson's motel room. They all knew that their dreams were about to come true. But how could they pass the time? They tried swimming, reading, watching TV, shopping at a nearby novelty store, and playing games. Nothing worked. Everyone was too wound up. They finally fell asleep, but not from being tired. It was sheer exhaustion that did them in.

Bright and early they were up and ready to go. No one wanted to eat breakfast. They were first in line to get into the parking lot and very close to the front of the line to purchase their tickets.

As they waited for the ticket booths to open, the people started to come from all directions. The Olsons had never seen so many people in one place. Many of them, already having their entrance passes, walked or ran into the park. Lines were starting to form. The Olson family shared a silent fear that there would not be enough room for them.

At long last they had their tickets and flowed through the gates with the growing crowd. They were in! Their dream was about to come true. Before long, they discovered that the long lines at the attractions moved quickly. They went from one attraction to another and loved every minute of it.

About midday, Jon started to feel overwhelmed. Ina and the children still had a lot of energy; he, however, was feeling the effects of the long drive, the pressing crowds, and the endless bombardment to his senses.

Ina sensed his discomfort. "Poor dear," she said, "you must be exhausted. Why don't you sit down for a while and rest? We would like to go back to a few things we have already seen. There's a bench in the shade over there. Go on over and take it easy. We'll come back and get you in about a half-hour."

Ina planted a kiss on his cheek before they all went off in their separate directions.

"I love you," she whispered.

"Bye, Daddy. See you in a little while," the kids called.

Jon went to the bench and was about to sit down when he noticed an alleyway that ran along the side of a French-fry stand and twisted out of view. There was no indication that it was off-limits to the public. In fact, a wooden sign with a black arrow was attached to the wall of the stand and pointed into the alley. Jon notice that no one was going back, and his curiosity was getting the best of him, so he decided to have a look for himself.

When he entered the narrow space between the buildings, Jon was surprised how cool and dark it became. There was something eerie about it all. He felt as though he was taking part in an old Frankenstein movie.

Deeper and deeper he went, leaving behind the noise and din of the park. He walked until he came into an open courtyard. It was a little brighter than the alley, but not by much.

Before him was what appeared to be a cave, and it looked much like the attractions he had left behind. Jon looked on his map for the name of this attraction, but he could not find it anywhere.

There were a few people there, but oddly, they were all adults. One by one they entered the open maw of the cave.

Jon noticed that something was written above the opening to the cave. He read: "Abandon All Hope Ye Who Enter Here?"

"Good effect," he thought. "If they want to frighten us, they have succeeded." Jon recognized the saying as being what appeared at the entrance in Dante's *Inferno,* but he didn't think that Dante's welcome mat had a question mark. "Hmmm, I wonder what that means?" he mused.

Something impossible to explain was drawing Jon deeper and deeper into the cave.

Not a soul was in sight. A recorded voice advised everyone to move to the left and make room for others. Jon laughed. He was the only one there. From the darkness a car attached to a moving belt appeared. The voice continued, "Please step onto the beltway and enter a car. When you are seated, the safety bar will come back automatically. Thank you, and enjoy your ride—if you can."

Jon wasn't sure he wanted to go through with this. He was surprised they would have anything this spooky in a theme park that catered to children.

Jon stepped onto the moving beltway and entered the vacant car. It was comfortable, and some of his misgivings started to disappear. The safety bar came back, the car turned, and it entered the opening in the wall in front of it.

He was plunged into absolute darkness. The car lurched and began to pick up speed. It spun, climbed, dropped, turned, and careened madly. Jon feared it was out of control.

After what seemed to be a long time, the car slowed.
Up ahead, a glow illumined the dark tunnel. Was it the
end of the ride?

A diorama came into view. The lifelike figures
intrigued Jon. But he gasped when he looked closely at
the display. There, in the diorama, was his family: Ina,
Ingrid, Al, and Inez. The scene was their home.

Jon recognized their living room: the worn sofa, the
old TV set, even the old, faded, artificial flowers in the
vase on the mantel.

Inez's voice came from a speaker behind his head.
"Where's Daddy?" she asked. "Oh, daddy has to work
late," his wife answered. "You know how important
daddy's work is to him."

"But we miss daddy," the children said together. "We
want him to come home to be with us."

Off to the side, in another part of the diorama, Jon was
at his office, working overtime again.

"I never thought that my job was coming between me
and my family," he thought. "I just want them to have
the things I never had when I was a kid."

Another diorama came into view. The scene was their
bedroom. The children were bouncing on the bed, and
Jon was trying to cover his head with a pillow. "Get up,
daddy," the children shouted. "It's time to get ready to
go to church." Ina's voice pleaded, "Come on, Jon,
there's not much time for your shower. We will be late
for church." From beneath the pillow, Jon mumbled,
"You and the kids go. I'm too tired. Maybe next week we
all can go."

From beside him came a strange voice. Jon jumped,
and his heart started pounding. An apparition of a
hooded figure sat beside him in the car, or, at least,
appeared to sit beside him. It said, "That's what you said
last week, the week before that, and the week before
that. In fact, it has been months since you went to
church with your family."

"But I'm always so tired," he began to protest but was cut short when the car he was riding in turned and he faced another scene.

Jon and Ina were in the kitchen. Jon sat at the table, their checkbook in front of him. Ina stood behind him, her hands clutching the top of his chair.

"But, there's nothing left over," Jon was complaining. "We can't afford to give anything to the World Hunger Appeal. We hardly have enough for groceries, and the cars need gas."

Ina looked sad. "We're not doing it right, Jon," she says. "We always give the leftovers. Can't we set a goal and give that first? Pastor Phil told us last Sunday that our gifts ought to be the first fruits. Giving is a matter of faith and priorities."

Jon slammed the checkbook shut. "Is that so? Well maybe Pastor Phil would want to come over here and handle our finances. If you or he has a better idea than mine you're welcome to the job of trying to make ends meet."

Ina cried as the lights went dim.

"Want to see more?" a voice asks from Jon's side.

Jon let out a yell. "Who are you? How did you get in here? You scared the wits out of me."

"How I got in here is not important. I just want to know if you want to see more."

Now Jon was angry. "What's the point of all this? Aren't all these things a bit exaggerated? I'm not that bad of a person."

"Oh, you're not bad, Jon. You just don't have your priorities in the right place. The direction you are going in will eventually take its toll. It is important to provide for your family, but not at the expense of your relationship with them. And your worship habits have become a bit sloppy. You could also use a refresher in stewardship. There's more, too. If you want to see them, we can look at them."

Jon shook his head. "No, I've seen enough. Now I understand the sign over the entrance. I guess there's no hope for me, is there?"

His companion laughed. "I can't get over at how slow people are. Didn't you notice: that was a question. You have an option. You can abandon hope if you wish. But you don't have to."

"Well, that's a relief. Maybe if I rearrange things, you know, spend more time with the family, be there for worship with them, and—"

"Now you've got the picture. I think you are ready for our final scene. You see, Jon, it's not that you have been so wrong. You live in God's Kingdom and that is built on relationships with God, with family, with others. It is also founded on service and many more things. But, I think you've got the picture."

"I do?"

"Yes. There's one more thing you need to see, and here it comes."

The car pivoted 180 degrees. Again Jon's family stood in front of him. They were accompanied by people representing other nations and races, and above them was an inscription: "Seek ye first the Kingdom of God and his righteousness and all these things shall be yours as well."

A warm feeling enveloped Jon. He felt good and complete. He turned to thank his companion, but he was alone.

His car picked up speed and was heading for a solid wall. Jon gripped the safety bar to brace himself for the impact. But it never came. Hidden doors swung open, and he emerged into the bright sunlight. Before him was a long line of people waiting to get on the ride, and in the front of the line was Ina and the children.

"Well, look who is here," she said to the kids. "Looks like daddy couldn't stay away from the excitement. And look at the ride daddy was on."

Jon turned and laughed. There above the entrance, emblazoned in huge gold letters was "Peter Rabbit's Wild Ride."

"Well, Mr. Adventure," Ina kidded, "how wild was it?"

Jon reached out, drew his family to himself, and held them close. "The wildest," he answered, "absolutely the wildest."

"When I survey the works of thy hands...the moon and stars which thou hast ordained, what is humankind that you should be mindful of them; or the children of humankind that you should visit them. Yet, you have made them a little lower than the angels." Burn these words in my mind, Lord, on my heart. Let me never surrender to hopelessness for you are my help, my hope, and my salvation. Amen.

Take Two Tablets and Call Me in the Morning

Theme: God's Covenant
Scripture: Exodus 20:1-17
Season: Lent; 3rd Sunday (B Cycle)

The people who had gathered at the foot of the mountain craned their necks as they watched the solitary climber slowly disappear from view. He was their hero. Women's hearts beat rapidly as they secretly fell in love with this brave man. Young children and teens idolized the seemingly fearless one who braved all kinds of hazards on behalf of those who were under his care. The men, at least some of them, felt safe and secure that he was the one to whom they trusted their lives. There were those who were jealous of his power and coveted his position of leadership; some even thought of clandestine ways to strip him of his reign. But, for the most part, these people slept soundly at night knowing that Moses was in charge.

The problem was, Moses did not share their confidence. In fact he was getting sick and tired of the whole operation. He had been up and down Sinai so many times that he used up all the liniment they brought with them from Egypt for his muscle cramps. It became so bad that when he saw the signs that the Lord wanted to talk to him again, Moses nearly broke down and cried.

This particular day seemed to be the straw that brought the whole load down. All the way up, as he carefully picked his way along the precipitous face of the mountain, he muttered to himself, "Why me? Doesn't He know how easy it is to ruin one's legs doing all this mountain climbing? I had to be picked by a God that had a thing for high places. He couldn't be like the one the Ammorites or Canaanites had. That one not only liked the valleys but she even enjoyed rolling around in the fields with the worshipers during their spring fertility rites. But not Moses. His God has to dwell on mountaintops. I should have known I would not be in for an easy time when I ended up talking to a bush."

Moses tripped. He caught himself just before he was ready to pitch forward and take a header.

"I knew I was in trouble when I came out of my tent and saw the mountaintop covered with smoke." That was the signal to Moses that the Lord had something to talk over. "Does He come down to me? No way Yahweh. He doesn't care how many sandals I wear out on this trail."

Just then a mighty bolt of lightning raced across the sky, followed by a roll of thunder that shook some good-sized rocks loose. Moses looked up and saw the smoke getting darker and thicker and glowing red from the holy fire. "Oh no," Moses said to himself. "It's going to be one of those days."

Moses trudged on and finally reached the summit. He sat down on what he had come to call The Meeting Rock and waited.

It wasn't long before the ground started to tremble and the smoke swirled in crazy patterns. Moses stiffened in anticipation of the first encounter. It was always unnerving.

The air crackled and became alive with static activity, and finally, the Voice.

"HI MOZE. WHAT'S HAPPENING?"

Moses cringed. First Aaron with this "Moze" business, now *Him*.

He was so fed up by now that if he had the courage he'd walk away, leaving the whole company of whimpering people in the desert, and he would spend a season on the Riviera. But one did not just walk away from the Lord without ruefully regretting it.

Again, the voice of the Lord rumbled. "HOW ARE THINGS GOING DOWN THERE?"

Moses waited before answering. He had long since learned that one must weigh carefully his or her responses to this One. He wrinkled his brow and said, "This is a trick question, isn't it? You really don't want to know how things are. Every time I told you before, you made things worse. When I told you they were hungry you sent manna. Do you realize what a problem you made for me with that one? You told me to call it manna. You didn't tell me that that word means "What is it?" Every time somebody asked me, "What is it?" I'd answer, "Manna," and they thought I was getting smart with them. And as if that wasn't enough, you sent manna in the morning, manna at noon, manna for dinner. And what did we have for a midnight snack to go along with our beer? Manna!"

"Then when we complained, you complied by sending quail: quail in the morning, quail at lunch, quail for dinner. You may bless us abundantly, but your repertoire is very limited. So, come clean. What is it you really want?"

"MOSES," the Lord answered, "YOU HAVE A WAY OF CUTTING RIGHT THROUGH THE CAMEL DROPPINGS TO GET TO THE HEART OF THE MATTER. SO, WE'LL GET ON WITH IT. I'VE NOTICED THAT MY PEOPLE (the Lord had taken to calling this wandering tribe "my people") ARE FLOUNDERING AND DO NOT HAVE TOO MUCH TO HOLD THEM TOGETHER. DISPUTES ARE BREAKING OUT. PEOPLE ARE GETTING INTO ALL KINDS OF TROUBLE. I THINK WHAT YOU NEED IS A SET OF LAWS. THAT WILL HELP IRON OUT SOME OF THE WRINKLES."

"Laws," Moses shouted, jumping up from his special rock. "We don't need laws. What we need is a place we can call home; some land to farm; good grazing fields for our livestock; a location where we can build our houses and put in some swimming pools. You might even consider giving us a few oil fields while you're at it. If this is asking too much, then at least get us some deodorant or a change of skivvies. The air is getting rancid down there."

The land trembled, lightning flashed, the smoke became more dense, and Moses said, "You're right, Lord, we need laws."

"MOSES," Yahweh continued, "I WANT YOU TO TAKE SOME DICTATION."

"Right," Moses replied, reaching inside his robe and pulling out a roll of papyrus, a feather quill, and some lampblack. "I knew I would need these someday. Just wait until I get everything spread out, and we'll have a go at it."

Everything became still. There wasn't even a whisper of a breeze, which is unusual because it was usually windy on the top of Sinai. The voice that spoke startled Moses because it almost sounded like an apologetic whisper.

"UH, MOSES, I WANT YOU TO WRITE THESE IN STONE."

"What!" shouted Moses, "In stone! Haven't you heard? We've got something new. It's called papyrus. Look." (Moses held out the material.) "This is what we use now. People haven't written in stone since the caveman days. Give me a break. In stone of all things."

"YES, MOSES, IN STONE."

Moses was really agitated. He started walking around in circles and flapping his arms up and down, which gave him the appearance of a downed gooney bird trying to become airborne. "Stone. Stone. There isn't even a stone around here flat enough to chisel on." At that moment a monstrous bolt came from the core of the swirling smoke and blew The Meeting Rock apart with a mighty blast.

"Now look at what you've done," Moses screamed. "You blew my seat to hell and back. What am I going to sit on when we get together? Now you've gone too far. I have half a notion—" Again the ground trembled. Moses stopped. "Right. In rock. I guess you want me to use these two slabs here," Moses said, picking up what was left of his seat.

"NOW YOU'RE USING THE OLD NOODLE," the voice affirmed. "I WILL DICTATE AND YOU START CARVING. NUMBER ONE."

Moses interrupted, "How many will there be, if it is not asking too much?"

"SUPPOSE WE START OUT WITH TEN. THAT SEEMS TO BE REASONABLE. NUMBER ONE. I AM THE LORD YOUR GOD. YOU WILL HAVE NO OTHER GODS. YOU SHALL NOT MAKE FOR YOURSELF A GRAVEN IMAGE OF ANYTHING THAT IS IN HEAVEN ABOVE, OR THAT IS IN THE EARTH BENEATH, OR THAT IS IN THE WATER UNDER THE EARTH. READ THAT BACK. I WANT TO SEE HOW IT FLOWS."

Moses read, "I am the Lord."

"IS THAT ALL? HOW DO YOU EXPECT ME TO
REMEMBER WHAT I DICTATE?"

Moses was just about at the end of his rope. He
responded sharply, "What do you want from me? Have
you ever tried to chisel a document into granite? Give me
a break. Maybe I can part water, but this is expecting too
much!"

"O, ALL RIGHT. STEP BACK."

Wham, bang, kazowee!

Light flashed everywhere, rock chips rained down like
a summer storm, and acrid fumes rose. Moses was
knocked flat, and when he rose he was covered with a
healthy layer of dust. "Give me a warning, Lord. You
nearly caught me broadside."

He looked at the stone slabs. Neatly etched in them
were the commandments. Moses began to read: "You will
have no other gods. You will not take the name of the
Lord in vain. You will keep and observe the sabbath day.
You will honor your parents.

"Sounds reasonable," he commented and continued.
"You will not kill. You will not commit adultery."

Moses paused. "Oh, oh," he said, "you might have a
little trouble with that one."

"DOESN'T MATTER. ADULTERY STAYS."

Moses shrugged his shoulders and read the remaining
laws. When he finished he picked up the two stone
tablets, which was not an easy feat because they weighed
about ninety pounds each, and he turned to get on the
trail.

"I'll take these suggestions—" more rumbling and
trembling— "right, commandments down to your people.
I know that they will be ecstatic to receive them. It's
what they have been waiting for with eager
anticipation." The note of sarcasm did not go unnoticed.
Just as he was about to start his descent, the voice called
once again.

"MOSES!"

"What now?" Moses asked.

"BE CAREFUL. I DON'T WANT ANYTHING TO HAPPEN TO MY COMMANDMENTS. THEY ARE IMPORTANT TO ME. I HOPE THAT THEY WILL OPEN A CLOSER RELATIONSHIP BETWEEN MYSELF AND MY PEOPLE."

"Are you kidding?" Moses countered. "They are written in granite. They are solid. If only tombstones could be so durable. Who could possibly break even one of them?"

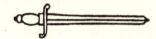

Lord of the Commandments, you have established the covenant of the law as a sign of your unending love for your children so that we, living in peace and harmony with you and one another, may enjoy the joy and hope of your kingdom. But I seldom see your law as a blessing. I make it a burden because I try to make my obedience the sole criteria by which you can love me. Help me to know that you have already delivered me from the land of slavery called sin; the house of bondage known as death. You have set me free to joyously live as your obedient child through your Son, Jesus. Deliver me, Lord, from myself. Amen.

The Dance

Theme: spiritual communion; special to God and one another
Scripture: 1 Peter 2:9-10
Season: 5th Sunday of Easter (A Cycle)

The gym at A.D. Greebley Junior High School was decorated with blue and white streamers, white and blue balloons, and a papier-mache eagle mascot. A record player in the corner scratched out a hit from yesterday, while couples awkwardly tried as yet unfamiliar dance steps. Boys and girls held each other at arm's length while dancing—except the basketball players and their cheerleader girlfriends. They danced close because they were supposed to. Athletes and cheerleaders have always been expected to be more demonstrative.

A large group of young people gathered around the refreshment table to drink fruit punch and eat crisp cookies.

The decorating committee had done a good job. They were able to transform the old gym into a respectable place to have a dance. The only things lingering that reminded those at the dance that this was a gymnasium was the smell of stale sweat and the basketball backboard and hoop. The aroma couldn't be covered, and the hoops had streamers hanging from them.

Philip hadn't wanted to come to the dance. He was there only because of the pressure from his friends—and his parents.

He was very shy. He did not know how to dance, and just the thought of holding a girl made him blush. Most of the time, he liked to be alone, reading or dreaming about being tall, strong, handsome, and popular. "Why didn't they mind their own business and leave me alone?" he silently complained.

Philip felt very awkward and clumsy. That is why he didn't even chance getting a glass of punch. He was afraid of spilling it and becoming the laughing stock of the school. So, he just sat on the bottom row of the bleachers, looking at his shoes, praying that no one would come to ask him to dance, and hoping his friends would leave him alone.

Anne didn't want to be there either. She was so self-conscious. Her dress was not in fashion, and she was sure that she stood out like a sore thumb. Most of the dresses she had were homemade and not at all like those that the other girls wore, the ones that were purchased in the best department stores in town. And she was starting to change—emotionally and physically—and didn't know what to think of these strange feelings. She often found herself thinking about boys, and she felt she looked awkward.

Anne also was afraid to dance. Oh, she liked dancing. But she was afraid that her partner would be able to dance better than she and would make fun of her or not want to dance with her again.

There was only one reason why she was at the dance. She had to get out of the house. Everything was so tense there. Her mother and father had been arguing a lot lately, and they both were yelling at her. If she had a quiet place to be at home, she would have been there. But, their house was too small and there was no escape.

So, Anne sat on one of the folding chairs that was standing against the wall opposite the bleachers. Every time a boy looked as though he was approaching her, she prayed he would pass her by, and her prayers were being answered.

That's how it was going for Philip and Anne that night at the dance. Both of them waited patiently for the dance to be over so they could leave.

For some strange reason—no one would be able to explain how or why it happened, it just did—the dancers parted, and Philip and Anne found themselves looking directly at each other. Their breaths caught at the same moment, and it appeared as though their gaze would be riveted together for the rest of the night. Philip was smitten by Anne's simple beauty, and Anne found herself attracted to Philip, though neither knew the other.

Philip wondered if he should risk asking her to dance. He thought, "She would never dance with me. She probably has a boyfriend. Besides, I can't dance. I'd only make a fool of myself."

On the other side of the dance floor, Anne was thinking, "It is too much to hope he'd ask me to dance. He probably thinks I'm ugly. Besides, he probably has lots of girls he'd rather dance with."

Philip and Anne never did dance that night. Instead they spent the evening imagining being together. Their imaginations made them the only ones on the dance floor. They were dressed in formal clothing and danced with the greatest of ease and utmost grace. They were the envy of the school. People standing on the sidelines pointed to them and called them the "perfect couple."

All too soon, the evening was over. The chaperones were saying something about how pleased they were at the behavior of the young people. Classmates started to file out and head for home or the nearest soda fountain. Philip and Anne were almost the last ones to leave. Their friends had to call them a couple of times before they even responded.

With their gaze still together, Philip thought, "Thank you for a lovely evening."

Anne said silently, "I had a wonderful time."

"Well, sport," Philip's dad said, "how was the dance?"

"It was great. I danced almost every dance," he answered, remembering the girl who sat across from him and their imaginary meeting.

"Oh?" his mother said, "Did you dance with anyone we know?"

"No, I don't think so."

His dad added, "If I know my sport, she was the prettiest one there."

Philip smiled, and blushed.

"I'm home!" Anne announced as she walked in the door.

"It's about time," scolded her mother. "Where were you? Did you come right home like I told you?"

Anne's dad threw his newspaper down. "Miriam, why don't you leave the girl alone for once? You are always after her. Back off a little." To Anne he asked, "Did you have a good time, princess?"

Anne just smiled and nodded. "I'm going up to my room. I'm tired. Good night, mother, father."

Anne slowly climbed the stairs, dragging her sweater behind her.

That night Anne and Philip went to sleep thinking about their night together at the dance.

I want to dance, Lord, but my feet won't move. I fear being rejected, turned down, and passed over. It is safer just to sit by the wall and wish I could dance. But you will not permit me to be a wall-flower. You call me; take my hand; move my feet until I am dancing to the music of your salvation. Amen.

Harold's First Client

Theme: the will of God; temptation; God in the midst of human strife

Scripture: Deuteronomy 6:4-6; Exodus 6:7; Luke 4:1-15

Season: Holy Trinity (B Cycle); 14th Sunday in Pentecost (A Cycle); 1st Sunday in Lent (C Cycle)

There is a resemblance between a dormant ant hill waiting to be warmed by the first rays of the springtime sun and the halls of an office building bathed in the gloomy grayness of the early morning hours. They both are quiet and empty but will soon be filled with the mad activity of workers rushing hither and yon—some with determination, others not quite sure what they are really supposed to be doing.

The hallowed halls of Brennan, Finch, Finch, Robertson, and Anderson, attorneys at law, were normally like that. But not on that one fateful morning when the new junior partner to the firm, Harold P. Quigley, was given the toughest assignment any lawyer ever considered.

Our story begins on one of those early morning, gloomy, gray days when the halls of office buildings are

empty...well, except for the back hall of the firm
mentioned above. There stood Harold. He was alone and
he was staring intently at a door. Really, he wasn't
looking at the whole door, just the new brass plaque that
had been attached by some maintenance people during
the night. Harold tilted his head this way and that to get
the best perspective of the lettering that was engraved
on the plaque. "Harold P. Quigley, Attorney at Law," he
read softly for fear that someone else just might be
somewhere in the complex and hear him.

He was proud of that plaque and the office behind it. It
had taken a long time, but he finally made it. So what if
he was only a junior partner to the firm and would be
listed as "and Quigley" whenever the secretaries
answered the phone. It was his office and he was proud
of it.

Harold took out his handkerchief and rubbed at what
appeared to be a fingerprint smudge. It wasn't a smudge.
"Damn," he said, "it is a scratch." He made a mental
note to find out who was responsible for the
workmanship and to see that he or she heard about their
ineptness.

Still grumbling about the scratch, Harold entered his
office. On the desk was a box that contained the contents
of his previous desk, which was located with all of the
others in the general pool. That place always reminded
him of a hospital ward. All of the desks were lined up in
neat rows and so close together that if you sneezed you
would blow the paper off the desk in front of you. There
was no privacy. If you happened to have a conference
with a client, you would have to reserve one of the small
conference rooms and hope that the person using it
before you would be finished on time.

He emptied the contents of the box. There wasn't
much in it. Harold was not one to collect a lot of things.
He was simple, rather plain, and very predictable. In a
few moments, everything was put away and the box was

placed on a shelf in the closet (he was going to keep the box for his next move—to a front office). Then Harold settled down in his padded chair, which he swiveled to look out of the window. The front offices had a view of the marina on the bay. Sunrise was always a spectacular sight.

Harold looked out over the back alleys and rooftops of the city. But instead of straight masts of sailing vessels, Harold saw bent television antennas. He could not hear the soft ringing of the channel buoy; all he heard was the mounting noise of the traffic and the rasping sounds of the city.

He turned his chair away from the window and gave out a yell of surprise. There, in the chair placed in front of his desk, was a woman. Harold's heart beat rapidly, but he wasn't sure if it was because of the scare of seeing her there or because of her sensuality. He had never seen anyone like her before. After a few seconds, Harold became aware that his mouth was hanging open and that the palms of his hands were sweating profusely. What was it that was so alluring about her? Was it her trim legs that were crossed seductively in front of her? The cleavage that was amply exposed by her low-cut dress? Her mouth that pouted in an exciting way? Her eyes that drew him in like the engulfing force of a whirlpool? Harold could answer only, "Yes, all of the above."

Harold cleared his throat, squeaked, and cleared his throat again. "I'm sorry that I just yelled. I didn't hear you come in, and you gave me quite a start."

"Think nothing of it," the woman said with a voice that turned Harold to jelly. "It happens all the time."

Struggling to gain some kind of composure, Harold diverted his attention by opening a drawer, pulling out a legal pad, opening the center drawer for a pencil, and slamming the drawer shut on his thumb.

The mysterious woman smiled as Harold tried valiantly not to scream with pain. It almost seemed as though she was enjoying his discomfort.

Suddenly a serious veil covered the face of the woman, almost changing her appearance. What had been exciting, gorgeous, and very sexy became cold and calculating, even a bit frightening. Harold knew from that moment on that she meant business and that no one really messed around with her.

"I want to retain you to represent me as my lawyer," she said in a no-funny-business voice.

Harold's mind was racing. "What could it be?" he thought to himself. "A divorce? Maybe she could be softened up as time went on, and then I can score with her."

Her eyes became black as coals, and Harold felt as though they were boring into his brain. "What is happening? I am starting to feel ill and dizzy," he thought to himself, praying that he would not become sick in front of this client.

As quickly as the sensation of illness came upon him, it left. She continued. "I want you to handle a lawsuit for me."

This was almost too good to be true. Not only representing what was probably the most beautiful woman in the world, but a lawsuit on top of it. That's where the big bucks were. If he was successful, his advancement in the firm would be helped.

"If you win for me," she went on, "you will be greatly rewarded."

"Now we are coming to the important stuff," he thought.

"Just imagine," she said, "being able to have your every appetite satisfied. No hunger of body or mind will go unfed. You will have enough wealth to do whatever you want and never be able to use it up. You will have security. Nothing will happen to you that you do not want. Nothing will ever stand in your way. And you will also gain power. Even being the head of this law firm will be peanuts compared to what you can have if you are successful in this suit."

"Wow!" Harold exclaimed. "You are giving me an offer I cannot refuse, aren't you? Aren't you exaggerating just a little?"

The sensuality returned. She slowly moved her head from left to right, indicating a "no" answer.

Harold leaned back in his chair and held the pencil between his two hands in front of him. "Who is it we are going to sue?" he asked.

"God!" the woman answered.

Snap! went the pencil as it broke in two.

Harold leaned forward. "What is this? Are you putting me on? Is this some kind of joke? Is this the way the senior partners welcome the new kid on the block? You were put up to this, weren't you? You have been pulling my leg all along, haven't you?"

"Don't you wish," she responded with an evil chuckle, licking her lips in a way that made Harold's Adam's apple bob up and down. "This is not a put-on. It is on the level. Win for me and you will be set for life. Pass this by and you will be able to kiss good-bye ever getting ahead," and leaning closer, "or ever getting anything you want."

"But, why God?" wondered Harold, "Whatever could we charge God with?"

"Simple," she returned. "We'll charge God with breach of contract. We can get the Lord for breaking the covenant."

Harold scratched his head (a nervous action he had developed). "I have a hard time believing you are serious."

"Oh, but I am. Read your bible and you will see where I am coming from. In Deuteronomy we read 'Hear, O Israel: The Lord our God is one Lord; you shall love the

Lord your God with all your heart, soul and might.' And
in Exodus it is further written, 'I will take you for my
people and I will be your God.'

A serious look clouded her face. She continued, "God
promises to be the God of his people. But, what kind of
God would allow people to suffer the way they do, or
wars to tear nations apart? I ask you, what kind of God
would turn away from poverty, hunger, or homelessness?
Is God keeping covenant when people are dying? No!" at
which the woman slammed her hand down on the top of
his desk with a loud smack.

Harold jumped and the parts of the pencil he was still
holding flew out of his hands. He bent over and picked
them up. When he straightened, she was gone. All that
remained was the haunting smell of her perfume. Harold
had never smelled anything like it before. It was both
pleasing and repulsive at the same time.

On his desk was an envelope. Harold's name was typed
on the front of it and the word "Retainer" was neatly
printed under his name. He opened up the flap and
gulped. There were thousand dollar bills in it. He started
to count but stopped after twenty-five. His head began to
swim. What was he to make of this?

He tossed the broken pencil into the wastebasket. He
still had a hard time believing what he had heard. She
had to be some kind of nut.

It was early in the morning, but Harold felt the need
for a drink. He walked over to the cabinet hidden in the
wall (don't all lawyers' offices have bars hidden behind
doors in the wall?). After opening the doors, he took a
glass, put some ice cubes in the glass, and poured a stiff
shot of scotch.

Swirling the ice in the glass, he turned and promptly
dropped his glass. Standing next to his desk was a little,
balding man. He wore a crumpled raincoat that was
open, revealing a suit that looked like it had been slept
in for weeks. What hair he had stuck out as though it

was charged with static electricity, and a burned-out
cigar stump was clamped tightly between his teeth in the
corner of his mouth.

"What's happening today?" Harold exclaimed, "Don't
people knock on doors any more? Who the hell are you?"

The pudgy little man held out his business card.
Harold took it and read: "Gabriel Angelico, R.O.Y.,
Trumpeter. Funerals, Weddings, Bar Mitzvahs.

"R.O.Y.?" Harold read out loud.

"Representative of Yahweh," was the reply. "Just call
me Gabe. Everyone else does."

Harold went to his chair again and sat down. "I must
be hallucinating. This can't be happening."

Gabe pointed to the envelope. "That pile of thousand
dollar notes isn't any dream, my friend. We have some
business to take care of."

Harold resigned himself to see this through to the end.
He picked up his pad on which he made some notes.
"OK," he responded, "if that is the case, then let's get on
with it. My client is charging your client wi—"

"I know," Gabe interrupted, "I know. We've been
through this all before, many times before. So, what do
you say we don't waste any time. I've got an
appointment to blow my trumpet at a special occasion
and I don't want to be late."

Gabe produced a shabby-looking satchel from which he
extracted what looked like a projector of some sort.
"Let's see, that wall over there should serve well
enough," he mumbled as he sat the machine on Harold's
desk, twiddled with some knobs, and threw a switch.

"Now," Gabe proceeded, "God is charged with not
being a very caring God." An image appeared on the wall,
a moving image. Harold recognized it as a battle scene.
He recognized Vietnam. The scene changed to Lebanon,
then Argentina, South Africa, Iran, Libya, street fights,
Ireland, mob killings, cocaine factories. Scene after scene
showed the present-day horrors of national, economic,

and social wars that are taking place everywhere. Harold
finally could not stand watching it anymore. It was too
terrible. "Enough," he said.

"Pretty gruesome, isn't it?" observed Gabe. "You can't
stand to watch it because it is against everything you
believe in. Well, my friend, Yahweh doesn't like it either.
In fact, you can't watch it because it stands for
everything that God abhors. He places in you and in
many others a moral conscience that cries out
"Enough!" against all of this inhumanity. Your client is
wrong for trying to get you to think God is responsible
for this. God wants an end to it, and your involvement in
striving for peace is an extension of God's work of
bringing creation back to its original order."

The scene changed to show the familiar pictures of
children with stomachs swollen from malnutrition, the
elderly sleeping under cardboard on city streets,
forgotten people in nursing homes, battered children,
abused wives and husbands, parched land... Again, it was
too much for Harold to take. He wished he had that
drink that the carpet had absorbed. But again the image
changed. People were shown at soup kitchens, eating a
warm and hearty meal; farmers were feeding other
farmers who had come to their aid during a serious
drought; buildings were being converted to house the
homeless; church members were paying a visit at a
nursing home. Image after image appeared, showing
people reaching out to help others in their plight.

"I get the message," Harold said, not giving his visitor
a chance to comment. "The problem is not an uncaring
God but one of uncaring people. We have the resources,
we have the food, and we have the means. All it takes is
the wisdom of love and distribution."

"Right," answered Gabe, "and Yahweh again is not the
one who abandons his people but continues to inspire

people like yourself to make a difference. God gives a damn! If the Lord didn't, the people of this earth would have wiped one another out a long time ago."

The scene changed one more time. It was the scene of a grieving family standing in front of a casket bearing the lifeless body of a family member. Other pictures of death and disease appeared in succession.

Then, a bright light filled the room. In place of what had been there was a cave, a tomb, the entrance of which was open. And in the background, on the top of a hill, were three empty crosses. From the bowels of the tomb emanated a brilliant light that filled the room with a warmth and security Harold had never before experienced.

"God is not the god of the dead but of the living." The voice was Gabe's, but Harold's heart spoke the words at the same time. "Jesus, God's only Son, came to bring light and life to all the world. Even though this physical life will come to an end, it is God's will that all the Lord's children will return and dwell in the presence of the Almighty. This is the Alpha and the Omega. God and God's eternal Kingdom, the New Jerusalem, is the beginning and the end. The resurrection of Jesus is God's 'No' to death's 'Yes.' "

Harold turned in his chair. "My client doesn't stand a chance, does she?"

Gabe chuckled and said, "Not a snowball's chance. She never did," he continued. "This is not a new challenge. It is as old as time itself. The rewards she enticed you with were used on one in a desert under similar circumstances. They have been used to turn the hearts and souls, yes, the dreams of every person whom Yahweh has claimed as his own. You would do well to forget all of those exciting promises because they all come with a price, and in the end you will have only that which she can give: death."

Harold started to laugh. "Do you want to know something funny? I don't even know her name."

Gabe nodded. "That figures. She didn't tell you," he said. "She never does. Her name is Satana. Satana Devilina."

Harold put his head in his hands for a moment. It was all too much to comprehend. He looked up. He was alone. "And you, my friend, you are the angel Gabriel."

But Harold was speaking to an empty room.

Was it real? Or was it a dream? The carpet had dried where the glass still lay on its side. The envelope of money was gone. Harold was confused.

Voices could be heard coming from the hall. Workers were coming for another day in the concrete anthill. He rose from his chair and started toward the door. As he passed the waste basket, he looked, and there, one laying upon the other on the black bottom, were the two halves of the broken pencil, lying in the form of a cross.

Lord, sometimes I do not understand your justice. How can you forgive people who work against you or love a world that is thumbing its nose at you? I am tempted to challenge your mercy, to question your economy, to dispute your wisdom. But to do so would be self-defeating. I may not understand your ways, and your thoughts are not my thoughts. But, thanks be to you that you are a God of love, and compassion, and divine justice. Amen.

The Vigil

Theme: dawn of a new age
Scripture: Matthew 17:57-61; Mark 15:42-47; Luke 23:50-56; John 19:38-42
Season: Easter Vigil

The setting sun cast long, thin shadows from the small group of people who, working against time yet lovingly and with adoration, were removing the lifeless body of their friend, lord, master, and savior from a cross. They paused only momentarily to allow a member of their troop to wipe a tear from his eyes with the back of his hand. Not a word was spoken about the guilt they all felt. Just a few hours ago, they had all fled for fear of their lives and had hidden in a secluded, out-of-the-way place while this one whom they followed and loved hung dying. They had no time now for remorse. The Jewish law was specific: No body shall hang upon a cross past sundown. Not only was dusk falling quickly, the Sabbath would begin as soon as night fell.

Nearby, a knot of women surrounded one who rocked back and forth as she wailed a lament for her dead

firstborn. The one common bond that held them together
in support and consolation was the love this crucified
one had for them and their love for him. He had taught
them well. He had prepared them for this moment. And
now that it had arrived, they remembered and reached
out to one another.

Peter, cradling the limp legs of the carpenter's son in
his arms, said to his brother, Andrew, who stood next to
him, "He had no house. He had no possessions. He had
no wealth. And today he dies without a tomb."

"Yes," responded Andrew. "Thank God for that
pharisee from Arimathea, Joseph. His generosity will be
remembered for many years. It is good that the tomb is
not far. We should be able to have our friend's body in
place before the Sabbath begins."

Peter nodded and shifted the weight he bore in his
arms. "But we will not have time to prepare Jesus for
burial as we should."

Nearby stood Mary, the one who was relieved of her
many demons and who paid honor to Jesus by pouring
her expensive perfume on him at the feast in Simon's
house. She overheard what Peter said, walked to him,
and lightly placed her hand on Peter's strong arm. "Do
not worry, my brother," she said. "The other women and
I will come early when the sun's light breaks the
darkness after the Sabbath. We will perform the ritual
for purification, anoint his body, and wrap it in burial
cloths. Let us make haste now. The time is passing
quickly."

The small cortege turned away from the crest of the
hill called Golgotha. They filed past the crosses of the
other two that were crucified that day. Fortunately, they
too had family to remove the corpses. Otherwise the
bodies would have been heaved over the brink of the hill
to land in the garbage heap where the carcasses of dead
animals were left to decay or be devoured by the birds
and animals of prey.

The tomb was within fifty yards of the site of the execution. With the utmost care, the body of Jesus was passed into the narrow opening and placed on the stone bed, elevated slightly at the head with a support at the bottom for the feet. Slowly, one by one, the disciples and the women backed out of the mourner's chamber, leaving behind the one who called them "friend."

Outside, soldiers waited impatiently. They had one more deed to perform at the request of the high priest. They rolled a large stone, a mill stone without the hole in the center for the beam, over the opening of the tomb and sealed it with a mortar-like compound. "There," one of the soldiers said. "That should satisfy old Caiaphas. Those disciples of his won't be able to get in and steal the body now."

"No," laughed another, and with a wink he said, "And *he* won't be able to get out either." Both laughed at the macabre joke and sat down under a tree to keep watch.

It was dark and cold and damp in the tomb. The soft scratching of insects that emerged from their hidden crevices filled the room with their eerie serenade. But all was still for a while, until the whispering began. At first it was soft and inaudible. However, after a time, the voices could be heard.

"This is my Son in whom I am well pleased." "Father, if it is possible let this hour pass from me."

"Lazarus, come forth." "He saved others but he cannot save himself."

"If you are the Son of God, command these stones to be turned to bread." "A man shall not live by bread alone but by every word that comes from the mouth of God."

"I and the Father are one." "Eloi, Eloi, Lama Sabachthani? My God, My God, why hast thou forsaken me?"

"Is this not the carpenter's son?" "Truly you are the Christ, the Son of the living God."

On and on the voices spoke, louder and louder, echoing in the stone vault—voices from the present, the past, the future.

"Woman, behold your son. Son, behold your mother."

"Before this day is over, you will betray me three times."

"Are you the King of the Jews?"

"Crucify him!"

"Abraham, get up and go to a place I will tell you."

"I have heard the cry of my children in Egypt."

"Repent and believe, the Kingdom of heaven is at hand."

"Here am I, Lord, send me."

"Our hearts are restless until they find their rest in thee."

"Unless it can be shown that I have gone against the precepts of Almighty God, I cannot, I shall not, recant. Here I stand. God help me."

"William, I baptize you in the name of the Father, and of the Son, and of the Holy Spirit."

The night was far spent and the new day dawned. Business went on as usual in the city of Jerusalem. The Jews kept their Sabbath. The Romans enforced their occupation. The non-believers sold their wares. Women bore their children; the dying gave up their last breath.

In the garden the guard was changed to keep watch at the tomb of the one called the King of the Jews. Finally, the Sabbath was over. The guards of the night before resumed their graveyard watch. For a while they amused one another with stories of how they had spent their day. Then, tiring of telling their lies, they drifted off to sleep. Just before the light of the new day started to cut through the sea of darkness, the soldiers were awakened by what seemed to be an earthquake. They jumped to their feet, standing at the ready for any trouble that might come. The ground continued to tremble under their feet. And then it happened.

Inside the tomb the voices were suddenly still. The dead, visited by the Messiah, had silenced their restless voices. The prophets had beheld the glory of their message. The witness of all that was, that is, and that ever will be had finally run its course. All was still. Even the soft scratching of the insects ceased. It was almost as if all of creation had paused in mid-course.

A light brighter than a thousand suns filled the sepulcher. In the midst of the light was a form, a form as of a man, and a voice: "YOU ARE MY SON. THIS DAY I HAVE BEGOTTEN THEE."

The earth trembled and the huge stone that sealed the opening to the tomb started to roll away. The darkness outside the grave was shattered by the light that shot out of the open maw and reached to the distant east to blend with the first rays of the third day. The soldiers were stricken blind and speechless, falling in near lifeless heaps, paralyzed by the wonder.

And the form, in the midst of the light, slowly walked to the entrance to the cave. He was no longer among the dead. He was living. He had risen.

For a moment he stood outside of the tomb. He smiled and looked up to heaven. Once again the heavens were filled with the heavenly hosts. Once again the Father stood at the very edge of the universe, eyes filled with the light of life. Once again the angels sang a hymn in praise of a God who is faithful to his promises.

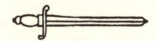

Christ is risen! He is risen indeed!

Footsteps in the Hall

Theme: hope, good news
Scripture: Romans 10:13-15
Season: 3rd Sunday in Lent (C Cycle); Festival of St. Andrew

No matter what you do, a hospital room will always be a hospital room."

That is what Marge thought as she lay back on the crisp, starched sheets of her recently made bed. She ought to know; she had spent enough time in hospitals over the years. Marge could trace the evolution of hospital rooms from the multi-bed wards that always smelled of disinfectant to the modern two-bed rooms painted or papered in decorator colors.

"Things sure have changed," Marge said to her comatose roommate. She knew that her observation would not be heard, but she longed for the sound of a human voice, even if it was her own.

"Look at this room," she went on. "We have two color television sets so that we can watch our own programs. The bed is motorized so that we can lift our heads or bend our knees just at the push of a button. A copy of a seascape is just where we can see it to give our room a more homey atmosphere. And, doesn't it beat all, our divider curtain has a floral print."

"But it is still a hospital room. Our beds have side rails to keep us from falling out. The controls for our television also has the call button that brings the nurses running when it is pushed. The nightstand hasn't changed much, and everyone knows that is where the bedpans and urinals are stored. And our over- the-bed tables still cannot be adjusted for comfort."

Marge let her head sink back into the soft pillow. She remembered her many trips to the hospital. Her first experience in a hospital was when she gave birth to her children. Then, as she became older, her gall bladder was removed. One year later she was back in the hospital again because of a ruptured appendix. Just last year she had undergone surgery for a hysterectomy. And now, now...

A worried look clouded her face. She tried not to think of it. But this was not something she could just pass off. Automatically her hand went to the bandaged area where she had first felt the lump. As much as she tried to reassure herself that it was nothing, she still felt the icy grip of the fist of fear on her heart.

She missed Paul. He was always such a comfort to her. She wished that he would be here with her now. The painting on the wall became a blur as she looked through tear-filled eyes, remembering her husband. But he was gone, and Marge was alone. Yes, she was alone, and that made her wait for the biopsy report all the more anxious.

She tried to direct her thoughts away from her fears, but she could not. Soon she was in dialog with herself. "I wonder how many people died in this bed," one side of her psyche thought. The other side responded, "Don't think about that! There were probably more who got well and went home." The negative side then thought, "Will I be in pain? Will I linger? Will I become a burden to someone?" "Fool," the optimist scolded, "you haven't even heard the results and you are already thinking the worst. You've had lumps before. They were nothing. This is probably the same."

And that is how Marge passed her time. She oscillated between gloom and hope. She talked to herself and listened. Marge listened to all the sounds that surrounded her and had become so familiar to her. There was the rhythmic "hiss, wheeze, click...hiss, wheeze, click" of her partner's respirator and oxygen. Looking at her watch, she thought that soon she should hear the sounds of the food carts being wheeled into her unit. She thought one of the casters must be damaged because it made a rattling noise as it was being pushed. Marge tried to put a face to the disembodied voice that announced seminars, paged doctors, and called "code blue."

Marge had a special gift. Her hearing was so acute that she could identify a person by the sounds they made with their feet when they walked. She knew which nurse was coming to take her vital signs; she could tell when her pastor was walking down the hall to visit her; she could identify which housekeeping person was mopping the floor outside her room—all by the sounds they made when they walked. She even knew the unique sound her doctor made as she hurried through her rounds.

Not only could she identify who it was, she could also tell whether they were happy or sad. It used to drive her husband crazy when she could tell what kind of a mood he was in just by listening to the sounds of his footfalls as he climbed the steps to the porch of their home.

Marge was jolted out of her daydreaming. She heard a familiar sound. She immediately knew who it was. Her heart skipped a beat. It was time. The sample had been taken and sent to the lab. Marge couldn't avoid it any longer. She felt her body surrender to the firm support of the mattress under her. It was her doctor coming with the results of her test. Was it good news, or was it what she feared the most?

She listened carefully. In a few brief moments, Marge's eyes again became filled with tears. She heard the voice of Dr. O'Connor as though it was coming from a time and a place far away. "Marge," Dr. O'Connor said softly, "I have the results of the biopsy."

"I know," Marge responded in a whisper. "I know. Please forgive me for crying because I also know what the results are. You came to tell me that the tests were negative and that I am OK. I'm OK!"

"How did you know?" Dr. O'Connor asked in amazement.

"How did I know?" Marge answered with a warm smile. "It was easy. I could tell by the sound you made when you walked. Your footsteps were happy."

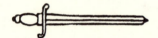

Thank you, Father, for those whom you have sent to bring the Good News in the midst of my fear and anxiety. The sound of their footsteps has lifted me beyond that which fills my soul with sadness. Send me as one who will bring glad tidings to those who await your word for them. Amen.

Bill's Christmas Eve

Theme: gift giving, Christmas, human drama and need
Scripture: Mark 12:41-44 (along with the birth narratives)
Season: Christmas

Bill leaned into the sharp December wind. In one hand he clutched the twisted paper handles of a shopping bag. With his other hand, he drew the collar of his topcoat tighter around his neck. "I don't remember a December as cold as this one," he thought to himself. The truth is, there had been colder ones. But, to Bill, this one appeared to be breaking records.

He was grateful for his warm coat. It may have been a bit too big for him, but Bill didn't mind. He was more interested in keeping warm than looking good. Many times, when he walked past the parish of St. Thomas, he offered a brief prayer of gratitude for the person who had donated the coat to be given to a needy person. Bill was one of the homeless persons that most people call street people.

"Good evening, Bill," called Officer Stanton, with a wave of his hand. "Merry Christmas."

Officer Stanton was a friend of the homeless. It was because of him that the city council agreed to open the old, abandoned railroad station to give shelter to the street people during the winter months. It was good to have a place that shielded them from the cold. The city even turned on the old steam system that was fed by the central heating unit. Bill and his friends would at least be warm.

They were proud of their shelter. Shortly after it was opened, each person was given a section of the big lobby as their own "territory." Each section was marked off by cots that were donated by a local service organization. The turf was respected by everyone, and all lent their hand to keep things neat and clean.

"Good evening," Bill responded. He did not, however, return the best wishes for a glad Christmas. This was not a very happy time for Bill.

Bill was torn between a number of conflicting emotions. He was so happy and proud to have his shopping bag filled with gifts for his "family" at the station. He was the only one that could afford to get these gifts. For about a month now, he had worked a part-time job. It didn't pay much, but he had enough to buy some half-decent food every now and then.

He smiled to himself when he thought of the day in November when he told his friends about his work. He was late getting to the soup kitchen set up in the basement of Salem church in the center of town. When he walked into the room, those who were already there took one look at his beaming face and shouted, "He got the job!" Bill had many pats on the back and well wishes. Even Mary gave him a hug. Mary never reached out to anyone before. She just kept to herself, silent and withdrawn.

The gifts that Bill carried home that night were not really all that much. They were all he could afford. There was a tube of lipstick for Mary; a tin of tobacco for

Harry; a comb and hair brush for Ellen; a pack of disposable razors for Ellen's "husband," Frank. There were twelve gifts in all. But Bill was most proud of the food he brought back. He had visited the kitchen of the department store where he was employed and had become close friends with the cook. All that day he set aside all of the untouched food that was sent back, and he put it in containers. At the end of the day, all of the food that was prepared but not sold was added to everything else. Now Bill and his friends were going to have a Christmas feast. Bill thought that he could even warm it up a bit if he sat the containers on the hot radiators.

Finally, to top everything off, he was able to buy some dinner rolls and a cake that were leftover in the bakery. With tomorrow being Christmas, the stores would be closed and neither the rolls nor the cake could be kept. The clerk rang everything up as "day old," and Bill got everything for very little.

It had been a busy day for Bill. His part-time work was very demanding. But he enjoyed it so. He especially liked the contact he had with people. Young and old, parents and children, married and single would smile when they saw Bill. Many people would wave to him and he would wave back. It was so good to be useful again.

They had a Christmas party at the store after shopping hours. Bill was invited but he did not go. It wasn't that he was ashamed of his clothes. He could have worn the uniform the store gave him to wear. No, it wasn't that. He just could not get himself into the spirit of the holiday. Bill felt very sad.

He arrived at the terminal. For a moment he paused with his hand upon the doorknob. He thought about the past two months. Faces of men, women, and children flashed in his memory. His heart became heavy, and he knew that he would have to release the burden before he entered the marble-floored room. He didn't want to spoil anything for his friends. They meant more to him than anything else in the world. Besides, he wanted to be happy when he gave them their gifts.

Still, he could not stop the one tear from flowing down his cheek. Bill sighed. It was now Christmas Eve and what meant the most to Bill was now gone. You see, Bill had been hired by Densers Department Store to be their Santa Claus—and on Christmas Eve, Bill and all other Santa Clauses all over the world lose their jobs.

But Bill had one more thing to do. He pushed open the door to be greeted by the smiling faces of all his dear ones. One by one he handed out his gifts, and one by one he received the only gift the others had to give: a warm embrace; a kiss on the cheek; a whispered "thank you."

Later that night, after the food had been eaten, the gifts opened, and the merriment spent, the lights were turned out, and the deep breathing of sleep echoed amidst the lingering call of train stops that were still held captive in the rafters of the station.

Bill lay on his cot and looked out of the window up at a cloudless, star-filled sky. He could hear the faint sound of the organ and voices of the Christmas Eve worshipers at St. Thomas Parish. He could picture the glowing candles; the choir and congregation; the priests dressed in their brilliant white with gold-threaded robes. Before he closed his eyes, he offered a prayer to a child who on this night was born in a place and situation not all unlike this one. That child is the one to whom all of this night was dedicated. It was to the glory of that child that Bill dedicated everything he had done.

Bill did not know it, but after he fell asleep, one bright, pulsating star shone on him through the night, keeping watch over one who had so little to give but gave it all.

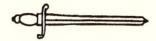

Lord, I have so much and give so little. Out of your love you gave all you had in your Son Jesus Christ. You gave him to us so that, believing, we will not perish in eternal death but have life. Show me the way to have less concern for myself and fill me with the knowledge that as we reach out to care for those in need we give praise to your Holy Love. Amen.

Father Eli's Retirement

Theme: Christ revealed through others
Scripture: Mark 1:9-11, 9:2-9
Season: Transfiguration (B Cycle)

Father Eli felt old and tired. And he was old and tired. Each day he expected a letter from his bishop informing him that he was retired from the active ministry and thanking him for his years of faithful service. It would be a form letter, but, thanks to the computer, it will at least look personal.

He was a good priest, a faithful priest. His ministry was never very spectacular. He never was asked to chair a committee, even though he served on many. His parishes were never large or wealthy. But that didn't bother Father Eli. None of that did. He just wanted to be there for his people when they needed him. The kindest thing anyone ever said of him was, "Father Eli always reflects his humble beginnings."

Born and raised in the small coal town of Jeddo, Pennsylvania, Elias Peter Moran witnessed poverty and need firsthand. He was the youngest of nine children. When Eli was eight years old, he came home from school

one day in April to a house full of mourning relatives.
His sister, Marie, the one he always felt closest to, took
him into the backyard and told him that his father was
killed that day in a mining accident.

Eli could not remember how long it took to recover his
father's body. All he could recall was the hastily planned
funeral and interment.

His mother worked hard to keep the family together.
One by one, his brothers and sisters found mates and
moved off to make their own way in the world. Elias was
not to follow suit. One day he said to his mother, "I want
to become a priest." The frail, tired woman looked at him
with warmth glowing in her eyes. "I know," she said, "I
have been praying for that every day since you were
born."

That's all that was said. That is all that needed to be
said. And now Father Eli was seventy-eight years
old—old and tired. And once again the same gnawing
fear ate deep into his soul. Was it worth it?

Just then the jangling of the phone shattered his
reverie. He answered quickly to beat his faithful
housekeeper, Theresa, to the draw. "St. Jude's," he said.
"Father Eli here."

"Father Eli," came the voice of the caller, "this is
Sandra Donovan."

Immediately Father Eli could see her: a small, sickly,
troubled woman who hardly missed a service. She had
been the subject of many of his own personal prayers. He
worried about Sandra.

The woman continued, "I just want to tell you how
much your homily meant to me this morning. You know
how worried I am that God finds it hard to love a person
like myself. Well, when you pointed to the bread and
wine and said, 'This is God's way of saying to us today,
"This is my Son," ' I knew as I never knew before that

God is a God of love and mercy. I still have a long way to
go, Father, but thank you. And, Father Eli, God bless
you."

The line went dead. And it wasn't until he hung up
that he realized that he hadn't said a single word after
he answered the call. He chuckled to himself. "Well
imagine that. Thank you, St. Jude. Thank you very
much."

He turned to the business before him. It was what he
liked least about being a priest. He often wished he
didn't have to worry about finances. So far, both the
church and the school were meeting their expenses, but
not by very much. And with his congregation growing
older, it would become harder for them to meet the needs.

After a while a soft knock came at the door. He knew it
had to be Theresa, and for her to disturb him he also
knew it had to be important. To get an appointment to
see the priest, a person had to go through Theresa, and
that was not easy because she saw her chief purpose for
being as taking care of Father Eli.

"Come," he called.

The door opened and Theresa came into the room.
"Father Elias," (she would never think of calling her
priest by the less formal title of Father Eli), "there is
someone here I think you would like to see."

She stepped aside and in walked a beaming young
couple. He recognized them immediately.

"Jim. Sally. What a pleasant surprise. Come in. Come
in." It was then that he noticed the small bundle Jim was
carrying in his arms.

Sally spoke. "Hello Father. We are in town for a visit
and wanted to stop by to say hello and have you meet
Robyn."

Father Eli took the small child in his arms. His heart
filled with joy the way it did every time he held a

newborn. He thought, "I know how Simeon felt when the Holy Child was placed in his arms. Every child is the embodiment of the Father's creative love."

They visited for a while. But seeing the work that still faced the old priest, Jim and Sally stood. This time it was Jim who spoke.

"Father Eli," he said, "Sally and I want to tell you how much it means to us that you went out on a limb a few years ago to marry us. You were our last resort. And then, when we found out that we could not have any children, you went to bat for us again and made it possible for us to adopt Robyn. We will never be able to thank you enough. You have showed us the compassion of Christ through your own love and concern."

They left soon after that. Father Eli had a hard time concentrating on the finances. The tears in his eyes made it difficult for him to see the numbers.

The rest of the day was fairly routine: meetings, hospital calls, and a funeral arrangement.

After supper, while relaxing with the one brandy and cigar Theresa allowed him to have, Theresa came into the sitting room. She wiped her hands on her apron.

"Father Elias," she said in a soft whisper, "a letter came today that I kept out 'til now."

She handed the envelope to the priest. It bore the bishop's crest.

He sighed. "Well, we know what this is, don't we?"

Theresa wiped a tear from her eye with the back of her hand. "Yes," she responded, "and it's a sad moment. But you do deserve a rest. You have worked so hard. You've been such a good priest. I never cease to be amazed at how patient you can be with some people, especially me."

Father Eli laughed.

"Many times," she continued, "I read the story of Jesus in the bible and I see a twinkle in our Lord's eyes—the same as the one in your own. I know others came to know their Lord because of you. But I want to tell you, when I came to work for you nineteen years ago, I was bitter and I did not believe. But because of you, my faith in Jesus has been restored."

She turned and left, leaving Father Eli with his unopened, computer-generated letter from the Office of the Bishop. He sipped his brandy and watched as the smoke from his cigar slowly rose toward the ceiling.

His soul had been troubled earlier that day, but now he could face the tormenting question head-on. Yes, it was worth it. To lead another to a firmer faith in the redeemer was a noble calling and worth every tear shed or pain endured.

It was then that Father Eli heard a voice echoing in his memory—a voice he heard many years ago when he was ordained a priest, a voice that spoke the message he promised to proclaim through his own words and deeds: "This is my beloved son. Listen to him."

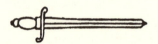

"O Lord, when did I see thee...?" Or is my prayer, "When did I reveal thee?" You have spoken to me through the voices of others: the glorious witness of the scriptures, the still small voice that calls my name in the middle of the night. I pray that I, too, have been faithful and that even in the smallest and most insignificant way, your name has been praised, your will accomplished, and your glory revealed. Amen.

The Front Man

Theme: preparing the way
Scripture: John 1:6-18
Season: 3rd Sunday in Advent (B Cycle)

He was a stranger in town. No one really knew when he arrived. One day he just was there. But, that's the way it always was. The front men came to town and left without much fanfare, and this particular one was no exception.

It was one of those crazy things. The people of Middleville always expected them. That's the way it had always been and that was the way it probably always would be. Summer after summer, at least one circus and three carnivals came to town. The folk of the small town always knew when they would be there. Posters would suddenly appear, directional arrows would be tacked to telephone poles, the grass in the huge empty field would be mowed, and the excitement would begin to run at fever pitch. On the day when they would arrive, all of the town's kids would gather at the railroad siding or at the field and watch them unload. Animals and wagons, tents and concession stands, trucks and trailers all formed a

long, strange, exciting procession that whet the
imaginations of children who dreamt of running away
and becoming a circus clown or carnival performer.

But first, before any of this happened, there was the
front man. He came under the veil of night. But you
could always tell when they were in town. They were,
well, different. They didn't dress like anyone else. They
didn't talk like anyone else. They didn't live like anyone
else. But they were always welcome because they
brought with them the promise of excitement. Young
people flocked to them to do chores for which they were
paid with complimentary tickets to the big show. The
front men met with the Rotary and Kiwanis and told
them of the wonders to come. Some even did a little
entertaining on the steps of the city hall: juggling,
singing, fire-eating and sword-swallowing. All the time
they would be surrounded by a sea of tiny faces that
watched with rapt attention, mouths agape, eyes riveted,
and hearts beating wildly.

And then this one came to town. He was a front man.
He had to be because of the way he was dressed. He came
with promise all but radiating from his person. He was
like all the others. Yet, in a strange way, he was
different. Some said it was the authoritative voice with
which he addressed the citizens of Middletown. Others
thought it was the wild look in his eyes—not wild in a
crazy way, but wild in an excited, committed sense.

He had his own bag of tricks, too. He did not juggle,
sing, eat fire, or swallow swords. Nonetheless, he
entranced the crowds that gathered around him. He had
a way of showing up when and where he was needed the
most and saying the right things that had to be said.

Like the time when a major feud was brewing among
the clergy members of the Council of Churches. It hadn't
come to blows, but it wasn't far from it. There was to be
a community worship service. First there was
disagreement as to where it should be held. No one could

remember where the last one took place, so every time a church was suggested, at least one or two of the members would not agree because they thought that was where the last community service was celebrated. Before that issue was resolved, the type of service was brought up for discussion. The Methodists wanted a loose, non-liturgical service, while the Episcopalians opted for a very formal service. The Lutherans wanted it to be a community communion service, and the Roman Catholics said they would not attend if it was. The Baptists wanted to bring in an Evangelist, while the Presbyterians knew of a college professor who was known as a good speaker. Well, tempers flared, voices raised, and fists pounded the table top.

It was then that one member suggested that the Council of Churches petition the Town Council to prohibit circuses and carnivals from stopping in their town because they were a bad influence on the young. It had nothing to do with the argument at hand, but that is the way it often happens in church groups—pertinent business is often ignored.

Well, that suggestion really divided the group into two camps. The argument intensified. But, almost mysteriously, the stranger in town walked into the meeting room.

The shouting mob of clergy hushed. The stranger stood at the head of the table, his eyes burning with fierce commitment. "Men of the church," he said in a low, deep, and commanding voice, "you argue over matters of such small magnitude while the major problems of this community go unaddressed. You worry about where you will meet to worship with no thought given to the people who have no place to live. You argue over the form your worship service should take while your community is filled with people who are starving spiritually. You fear

for the influence upon your young while you lock
yourself up in your ecclesiastical towers. If you want
your community to change, you must change yourselves!"

As quickly as he appeared, he turned and left. The
Council of Churches felt chastised. Some resented the
brashness of this newcomer. Most, however, knew that
he was right and that they did spend far too much time
on trivial things while the important needs went
untouched. After that day a few quit the ranks. But
those who stayed on and toughed it out started a whole
new ecumenical outreach to meet the physical and
spiritual needs of the small town.

He was a front man. And a front man always prepares
the community for something greater to follow. Most of
the people wondered about what was to follow. A few
times he was asked, "What are you preparing us for?
What comes after you? A circus? A carnival?"

The stranger would answer their questions with a
smile. His eyes would light up with excitement and he
would say, "What comes after me is far greater than
anything you have ever seen or heard. It is so wonderful,
I cannot even find the words to talk about it. Even the
things that I did while I was with you are nothing to
what you will see and hear."

And so it went for many days. People still disagree as
to how many days the stranger lived in their midst. But
it really does not matter. Most people remember this
front man for the last evening he spent with them. They
were all gathered near the town line. He called a
gathering of all the people, and they came. At least, most
of them did. The disgruntled ex-members of the Council
of Churches did not show up, but that was to be
expected. Some brought lawn chairs. Others spread
blankets out on the ground. A few even brought picnic
baskets with food.

He stood before them and the crowd was immediately
silenced. He said, "I have come among you to prepare the

way of that which is to follow me. Together we level the
hilly place and make the highway straight. You wonder
at my words. The one who shall follow is even mightier
than I am. Prepare yourselves. Repent!"

He turned his back to the crowd and started to walk
away. He stopped, turned, pointed his finger
heavenward, and said, "Behold the Lamb of God, who
takes away the sins of the World!"

And then he was gone. Life went back to normal after
he left—well, as normal as it can be when people start
caring about people. He was a stranger in town. No one
knew when he had arrived. But one thing everyone
agreed upon: There had never been nor will there ever
again be a front man like John.

*Dear Lord, so many things in my life crowd you out. It is
not that I willingly fill all my space with other things. It's
just that I do not make the room; I do not hear the voice of
your forerunner, the front man, calling, "Make ready the
way of the Lord." I spend my time making many prepara-
tions. Now I want to prepare a place for you. Come into my
heart, Lord Jesus. Amen.*

Harry's Day Off

Theme: labor; Sabbath; rest
Scripture: Exodus 20:8-11
Season: Labor Day

Harry used to feel guilty for all of the time he put in at the office. He knew that Nancy was at home with the kids: slaving at the same routine day after day, week after week, not really having much satisfaction with cleaning the house, doing the laundry, changing messy diapers, and trying to salvage one more meal that was being kept warm in the oven for hours. Which reminded him, he forgot to call Nancy and tell her that he would be late again. "Oh well," he rationalized, "I am doing it for them. If we want to have all of the things that are important to us, I will have to keep putting in this overtime. Anyway, someday I will be able to give all of this up and then spend time with my family. I will make it up to them then."

He closed the file that was in front of him and put it to the side. Harry knew that Sheila, his secretary, would be in first thing in the morning and that she would return the folder to its proper place. "Thank God for good secretaries," Harry said to no one special. "I don't know what I would do without Sheila." And Harry was right. He was an excellent manager, well on his way to becoming a vice-president of the Hastings Fabrication Corporation. But he didn't have the foggiest notion of how to operate an office. The filing system was a maze to him, and he knew enough to let those who understood it do their work.

He picked up another file from the large pile that was placed on the left-hand edge of his large desk. He opened it and started to read. He stopped and reread the information. A worried look creased his brow. Turning in his chair, Harry leafed through some papers in his briefcase until he found what he was looking for. He placed it next to the one he was reading and compared the lists of figures on the two sheets of paper. Slowly his face became beet red. He clenched his fist and brought it down on the top of his desk with thundering force. "No!" he shouted, "That idiot has screwed up another account. That's it. Tomorrow morning he goes. I cannot tolerate his incompetence any more."

Without warning a sharp pain caught his breath. It was as if a hot knife had been thrust between his shoulder blades. His left arm carried the signal of pain as it radiated to his finger tips. He could hardly breathe. He stood, tried to loosen his tie, and lost consciousness.

The pain was gone. That was a welcome relief. Harry couldn't remember ever having anything like that happen to him before. In fact, with the pain gone, Harry felt rather good; almost as if he was next to being weightless. Yes, that was it. He had a floating sensation.

Then Harry realized what had happened. "Oh no," he cried, "I am going to that big corporation in the sky." He giggled a little at this, but he soon sobered. "What will become of Nancy, and the kids? Sure, I have a lot of insurance, but the mortgage on the house and payments on the boat will eat that up in no time at all. There won't be enough to send Jason to college or pay for Meredith's wedding, or..."

Harry started to cry. He couldn't remember the last time he had cried. It was a strange feeling. There was a bitterness, yet a release; yes, almost as if someone was lifting a heavy weight off of his chest.

"Was it worth it, Harry?" Harry's heart pounded harder at the sound of the voice. He hadn't expected it. No one was there. Then again, no one had to be there. Harry knew what was happening. He knew where he was.

"Well," the voice persisted, "I am waiting for an answer. Was it worth it?"

Harry thought a while. Finally, he said, "At the time, I thought it was. I wanted my family to have everything I didn't have. You know what it was like when I was a kid. All the other kids in the neighborhood had things that were bought in stores. Most of the toys I had, Dad made. I was embarrassed that we couldn't go to the store and buy what we wanted. The only thing we had was a close relationship in our family. We used to play games, go on picnics, and take walks. Well, that wasn't enough for me. I made a vow that when I married and had children, my wife and kids would not have to want for anything. They would have anything they wanted."

"Except a father," the voice added. "I am sure you see what happened, don't you? Your wife and children not only don't have you now, they didn't have you before. You turned your labor into a curse for them. Do you know how many times Jason cried because he wanted you home to play with him; or how many times Meredith wished you could tuck her into bed and kiss her good-night; or how many times Nancy wanted you there, just to talk, to hold her, to spend a few quiet moments with her?

"Work was meant to help a person provide for the necessities of life. The fruit of your labor was to provide for your needs. But your needs and the needs of so many other people have become confused with their wants. You wanted a house in the suburbs; Nancy needs a home and family. You wanted toys for your son; Jason needs a father to play with him. You wanted the best school for Meredith; she needs you to listen to her hopes and dreams, her fears and doubts. And you wanted to climb that ladder of corporate success when what you really needed was simply to work to provide and to rest and to be a good husband and father. And, if I may add, to worship, which is something you have been neglecting to do."

By this time Harry was sobbing uncontrollably. So much time had gone by and now it was probably too late. "I don't want to die. There is too much for me to make up for. I want to be with Nancy and the children. I want to be there when they grow up. Oh, I don't want to die."

"Who said anything about dying?" the voice asked. "Right now the paramedics are wheeling you into the hospital. You can thank old Jake, the janitor. He was outside your office when you fell across your desk and knocked the aquarium to the floor. He called the emergency unit, but is he mad at you for the mess you made." Harry heard a soft chuckle. "Go back now, and remember, your work is important. But put it in the right perspective. Master your labor and do not become its slave. Think back to your religious school days. You memorized the commandments. Take them all seriously, but especially the one about work and rest. Do your labor. But you must also take time to be revitalized. And remember that it is also important to worship. Through your work, worship, and rest you are to be strengthened and comforted. The Sabbath is my sabbatical; it was meant to be yours as well."

The voice had become fainter and fainter so that Harry had to strain to hear what was said at the very last.

"Harry, Harry," someone was whispering. The voice was soft and sweet, like that of an angel. He focused his vision with some difficulty. Slowly he was able to make out the tear-filled eyes of Nancy looking lovingly at him. She was softly stroking back the hair on his head. "Welcome back, darling," she said, biting her lower lip to keep from breaking down. She took his hand and held on with a fierceness Harry had never known before. "You've been out so long. I was afraid—" Nancy couldn't finish.

Harry held up his hand. "It's all right, sweetheart. I'm back and I think I'll stay for a while." He looked around the room. He was connected to an intravenous feeding tube; over to the side an oscilloscope recorded the pattern of his heartbeat. White- uniformed people hurried by his open door. "What day is it?" he asked.

Nancy smiled and said with a soft whisper, "Sunday. It is Sunday."

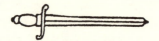

Eternal Creator, you have made all things good and wonderful. Why do we abuse them? Why do we drive everything we have to the brink of destruction? You have made us in an amazing way. In your infinite wisdom, you have set our minds and hands to useful work. But you have also commanded that we practice good stewardship over this gift of life, and part of that responsibility is to strengthen our labor with re-creative rest. Help me to see that in the balance of nature you have also provided for the care and nurturing of ourselves. Help me to remember the Sabbath Day and keep it holy. Amen.

The Peace Giver

Theme: peace making; giving; keeping
Scripture: John 14:27
Season: 6th Sunday in Easter (A Cycle); Festival of Sts. Simon and Jude

The last time Jim could remember feeling so out of place was when he went to his wife's high school graduation reunion. He hadn't known anyone there, and no one seemed to want to be honest. His wife, Connie, knew that he had not enjoyed that evening very much. Nonetheless, she was grateful that he had endured the experience. She was proud of Jim, and it had been a pleasure introducing him to those who were her school friends, and showing him off to those who weren't.

Now, again, he felt as though he didn't quite belong where he was. The 8th Street Armory auditorium was filled with people, and he didn't know one of them. A cloud of uneasiness hung over the crowd. There was a lot of milling about, but an eerie silence prevailed—almost as if everyone had something to say but no one wanted to start the conversation. "Maybe they don't know why they're here either," Jim thought as he wondered why he

67

had decided to come to this meeting. Was it because his
curiosity got the best of him? Or was it because the
announcement he received read more like marching
orders than an invitation?

Jim took the worn letter from inside the breast pocket
of his suit. He had read it so many times he knew it by
heart. Although he had received it less than a week ago,
it was showing signs of wear from being folded and
unfolded with frequency. He read it again:

Mr. James Larsen
1310 Elm Drive
Kadel, PA

Dear Mr. Larsen:

*Your presence is expected at an urgent assembly of
persons that will be held in the 8th St. Armory on
Wednesday, May 26, at 10:30 a.m. The purpose for
this event will be explained at the meeting. Please
use the main entrance and proceed directly to the
auditorium. Please be there, and again note that the
meeting will begin promptly at 10:30 a.m.*

The New World Coalition

There was no R.S.V.P. number, and Jim had checked
the envelope many times to make sure he did not miss
the response card. "Do I have any option?" Jim
wondered. "I don't see that I have a choice."

At first he resisted even thinking about going to the
armory on Wednesday. He had served four years in the
army and lived by following orders. Now he was his own
boss and he took orders from no one. When he received
his discharge papers, he made a vow that he would not
let anyone ever make a decision for him again. This
letter not only reminded him of his promise to himself,
but it brought back memories of a time when he knew he
had no control over his own life. "Nobody is going to tell

Jim Larsen what to do," he proclaimed to Connie, "and I'll be damned if I will go to that meeting. The New World Coalition can go to hell."

Connie knew Jim, and she also knew that it would be best not to say anything. She had heard this speech many times before. "He'll go," she told her friend Sally. "He always blows off steam, but he's soft, and curious."

She was right. For all of his grumbling and complaining, Jim was at the armory well before the prescribed time. He thought about the work that was waiting for him at the office; the nerve- racking commute to the city; and the bag lady he had encountered outside the armory.

"Please, sir, can you spare some money for food?" she had pleaded as she held out a grimy hand.

Jim had shaken his head gruffly and walked by without so much as looking directly at her.

He thought, "Those people are a nuisance. Why can't they get them off of the street? Money for food, indeed; for a bottle of cheap wine is more like it."

He looked at his watch just as the LED numerals changed from 10:29 to 10:30. The double doors at the other end of the auditorium opened. All eyes turned to the open doors as a large group of people walked into the spacious room and formed a human corridor that divided the room in half. A murmur of wonderment rippled through the people who had been waiting, and Jim became apprehensive at this impressive entrance. That they were all dressed identically did nothing to diminish his concern. Now more than ever he wondered why he had bothered to respond to the invitation, and he had to fight hard to resist a temptation to leave. But again his curiosity won, for he did want to find what this was all about.

The new arrivals turned with military precision and faced the open doors. An extremely bright light flowed through the doors into the auditorium. A figure could be seen approaching the assembly. At first Jim could hardly make out a faint silhouette. But before long, the full feature of a man walked through the doors and mounted the steps to a small, hastily assembled stage that had been erected.

Jim had a hard time recognizing any distinguishable features of the person occupying the stage. Although there was no evidence of a spotlight, the figure was bathed in brilliance.

The auditorium was absolutely quiet. Those assembled knew that they were about to be addressed by the person in front of them. But he slowly let his eyes move over the faces of the crowd. When his eyes met Jim's, Jim felt his pulse and breathing increase. He was filled with a strange sense of electric excitement. Finally, after what felt like a long time, the stranger spoke.

His voice, though not loud, filled the room. It was rich and soothing while commanding attention. Not a person moved, no one coughed, and it is altogether possible that no one breathed.

"Friends," he began, "thank you for coming. Your presence here is of the utmost importance in the history of human kind. We apologize for our dramatic entrance and hope that our number does not fill you with anxiety. Believe me when I tell you from the very first that we represent the greatest good.

"You are probably wondering who I am. For now, let me introduce myself as the Peace Giver. If you know me by that title, you will be able to fully understand why it is you were summoned to be here today and to become a part of our company.

"Which leads me to why you are here. You have been invited to receive what I have to give—Peace—and when you have received it, to become, along with the rest of my company, the Peace Keepers.

"First, let me explain what I mean by 'peace.' You know it mostly as the absence of strife. The way this is

achieved is by overcoming all others and, through
continued power and might, enforcing this absence of
conflict. The problem with this is that there is always
someone who is trying to become more powerful, and the
prevailing controller is often challenged. Peace,
therefore, exists as long as one power can keep all other
powers under its control. You have often in your history
used the term 'Peace Maker.' A peace maker, by your
definition, is one who succeeds in prevailing over others:
by might, by thought, by suggestion, by leadership, by
influence. Whatever it is, that peace is fragile.

"I have a different peace to give. It is not the absence
of strife or conflict. It is, rather, a relationship. The
ancient folks had different names for it. The Hebrews
called it 'shalom.' The Greeks used the word 'eirene.'
This peace does not depend on a strong power
maintaining it. It happens as people live with each other
in a relationship of love, concern, justice, hope, and
shared resources.

"That, briefly, is why we are here. I cannot tell you
everything. Most of what you will learn will come by
experiencing it. I am the Peace Giver. You will all come
before me to receive it and you will be my Peace Keepers.
But to keep my peace, you must use it, even give it away.
Don't worry about how. That will be revealed to you in
time."

A line started to form in front of the stage and
continued between the two rows that formed the human
aisle. One by one those in the auditorium stepped in
front of the speaker. He leaned toward each person,
placed his hands on them, and said something. His voice
could be heard above the slow shuffling of the feet, but
Jim could not distinguish the words.

After a while, Jim found himself in line and slowly
moving toward the stage. When he looked at the people
on either side of him they looked backed and smiled
warmly. Of one Jim asked, "Who is he?"

"Why, he's the Peace Giver," came the smiling reply.
He asked another, "What will I be expected to do?"
The reply was "Don't worry, friend. You'll know when
the time comes."

Slowly the line moved forward, and as Jim got closer
he was overcome by a feeling of uneasiness. "I still don't
know who he is or what this is all about."

But before he could make up his mind to turn and
leave, he was standing before the central figure in the
room. The man smiled at Jim. Again Jim's heart raced.
"That face," he said to himself, "it is filled with such love
and understanding."

The man on the stage motioned for Jim to move closer.
It was then that Jim noticed for the first time the scars
on the speaker's brow and the marks of the wounds in
his hands.

Jim turned and looked back. "Why, he's—" Before he
could finish, one of those who entered with the speaker
nodded his head.

Again Jim faced the Peace Giver. The speaker leaned
forward and place both hands on Jim's shoulders. He
looked deep into Jim's eyes and said, "Peace I leave with
you. My peace I give to you. Not as the world gives do I
give to you. Let not your heart be troubled, neither let it
be afraid."

Jim tried to respond, but all he could whisper softly
was, "Thank you." He turned and walked away, hardly
aware of anyone around him. If he had not known better,
he would have thought his feet were not touching the
ground.

The meeting was over for all of those who had received
the blessing of peace from the Peace Giver. Now they
went into the world as the Peace Keepers, filled with a
new sense of understanding and purpose. No longer was
power, or success, or influence, or advancement
important. They had a new mission.

Jim left the 8th Street Armory as one who had been touched by the presence of the Prince of Peace.

"Say mister, are you sure you don't have any money for a meal?"

Jim looked and there before him was the same bag lady with grubby hands held out to receive whatever Jim would give her.

"Funny," Jim thought, "she is not the same person I saw on the way in. There is something different about her."

"No," Jim answered, "I don't have any money for a meal. But I have something better than that. Come home with me, and my wife and I will give you a good meal. Stay with us until we can find adequate housing for you and some support so that you can have a warm place to stay and three decent meals a day. If we can't find such a place, we'll shake the bushes until someplace can be established for you and your friends."

"Do you mean that, mister?" asked the lady.

"Sure do!" exclaimed Jim. "Why don't you gather up your things and bring them with you. Here, let me give you a hand."

Jim turned and looked back at the armory and saw, standing behind the glass doors, the smiling face of the Peace Giver.

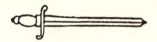

O Lord, Prince of Peace, you give me the gift of peace to keep and to use. You are the shalom of my life and I pray that I can be that for others. Fill me with the peace that passes all understanding so that my heart and life can be kept in you, Christ Jesus, my Lord. Amen.

Liberated and Set Free

Theme: freedom
Scripture: John 8:31-36
Season: Lent; general

Gene's cell was damp, dark, and musty. He had been a prisoner for more years than he could remember. And as each day passed, the rays of light from the outside grew dimmer and dimmer. Gene was beyond hope, yet he could not allow himself to become accustomed to the dungeon in which he was chained. Day after day, night after night, he cried out for help, but no one heard.

His imprisonment brought hardships beyond imagination. The gruel upon which he fed daily was bland and tasteless. Vermin were his constant companions. But it was the loneliness that was most oppressive. "How long has it been since someone has set foot inside my cell?" he wondered aloud, startled at the sound of his voice. At times he heard movement outside the door of his cell, but when he called out, no one would answer. Three times a day food was placed just inside the

74

door to his cell, but never had Gene seen the bearer of the gift, for it was pushed into his cell through a small panel that opened near the bottom of the door.

Gene had to fight madness due to the terrible boredom. His only companions were his thoughts and memories. "If only I could remember the good things!" he would say many times during the course of the day. "What does a field of ripe wheat smell like?" he wondered. Taking a deep breath he inhaled the pungent smell of mold and mildew. "How does sand warmed by the sun feel on bare feet? What does it feel like being embraced by one's lover?" All Gene could do was wonder. His feet did not feel warm sand but damp stones. Lover's arms did not embrace him; only his loneliness held him in its tight, relentless grip. He heard not the sound of a child's laughter, a brook's song, or the wind's whisper. He only heard his inner voice remembering, remembering, remembering.

One day, as he walked the endless path that encircled the perimeter of his cell, he heard the sound of the panel in the door being slid back. "That's strange," he said to a spider that shared his enclosed space, "it's not time to eat. Why was the panel moved?"

He looked over to the door and noticed a small piece of paper laying on the floor. Gene picked it up, unfolded it, and saw that it was a handwritten note. He trembled as he read the message. This was the first communication he had with anyone since he became a prisoner. He savored each word. The note read: "I have seen how cruelly my people are being treated...I have heard them cry out to be rescued...I know all about their sufferings, and so I am coming to rescue them. Exodus 3:7, 8."

Gene didn't understand. What did it mean? Who sent it? He turned the paper over, hoping there was more; there wasn't. He held the piece of paper with the cryptic message for the longest time. Then he crumbled it up into a small ball and threw it onto the floor.

"It's just their way of tormenting me," he fumed. "It is not enough that I have to endure my own agony; they must add to it. What hopes do I have that anyone cares enough to rescue me? I have been here too long for anyone to notice."

And so, Gene sank deeper into his dark depression, making the walls of his prison thicker still. Day seemed to flow into day. The little wad of paper stayed in its place for the longest time until one day it was gone. "All well and good," Gene observed, "it was only another bad memory for me. It is probably lining some rat's nest by now. That's about the best use for it."

Just then the panel moved again, and another folded note was put in front of the door. This time Gene did not run to pick it up. In fact he debated for the longest time, wondering if he should or would. Finally, more out of curiosity, he bent over, picked it up, slowly unfolded it and read: "God loved the world so much that he gave his only Son, so that everyone who believes in him may not perish but have eternal life. For God did not send his Son into the world to condemn the world, but to be its liberator. John 3:16-17."

Memories of bygone days flooded into Gene's consciousness. He remembered the feeling of wonder and release when, after confession, he would hear in the words of the absolution, "I forgive you all your Sin, in the name of the Father, and of the Son, and of the Holy Spirit." He remembered when, after a bitter argument, he would collapse in his wife's arms and say, "I'm sorry." No kinder words did he ever hear than, "That's OK, I forgive you." Wave upon wave of memories washed upon the shore of his mind, bringing back the remembrance of sin confessed and forgiven. And in the wash of each wave, he heard, "Repent and believe. Go and sin no more."

Shaken by the force of the tide of memories, Gene called out at the top of his voice, "God, be merciful to me,

sinner that I am. O Lord, I believe. Help me in my
unbelief." When his words ceased to carom off the walls
of his prison, Gene collapsed and fell against the door of
his cell. When he did, it swung open and he stumbled
into the blinding light of freedom. His body and soul
were bathed in the warmth of a long forgotten awareness
of love and joy. Hope once again rose like the water of an
artesian well. He was liberated; he was free.

Gene turned and looked, perhaps for the last time, at
his prison. It was a dungeon built out of his guilt and
shame, from which he once believed he could not be
freed. The walls were made thick and impenetrable
through the years of holding at arm's length any word of
good news about God's offer of salvation. He had fed on
the gruel of self-pity and had existed among the vermin
of sins that were thought to be too severe to be forgiven.
And, most tragic of all, the door of his cell was never
locked. It stood open, waiting to receive the weight of a
soul that cried out to a God who sees how cruelly people
treat themselves when they do not lay their sin and guilt
before Him; who hears the cries of those being driven by
the whips of that which holds them as slaves; who knows
their suffering and who in Jesus Christ comes to rescue
them.

What is it that freed Gene? It was the truth. "If the
Son sets you free, you shall be free indeed!"

*Gracious Lord Jesus Christ, you have come to set your
people free; you have heard their cries; you know their suffering. Release me from that which holds me in bondage.
Liberate me from my slavery to sin. Break down the doors
to the prisons in which I hold myself captive. Fill me with
the truth of your saving grace so that being freed by you, I
may be be truly free indeed. Amen.*

Carmen's Holiday

Theme: Thanksgiving
Scripture: Ephesians 5:20
Season: Thanksgiving, 6th Sunday in Pentecost
(C Cycle)

C armen appreciated the time alone. The nurse's
lounge was empty, so she could have a few
moments to prepare herself for the shift that was
ahead of her.

She liked her job at Central Hospital. The rewards of
the smiles from the patients made the sacrifice and the
expense of going to school worthwhile. She was proud of
her accomplishments, and now all of the hard work was
paying off.

Carmen looked at the image being reflected in the
mirror before her. She tried to wipe away a few of the
wrinkles that appeared in her fresh, white uniform. She
saw that she was indeed as attractive as many told her
she was. Her face glowed as she smiled thinking of the
effect she had as she walked past a group of interns.

Then, looking straight on, she saw the identification
badge she had to wear. "Carmen Sanchez, LPN" was

typed above a polaroid picture. That pin said it all. Now, having successfully reached this goal, she was ready to set her sights on another. In just a few years, after attending night school and taking the exams, she would be able to trade her LPN for an RN.

Usually Carmen was anxious to go to work. But today she did wish that she hadn't had to leave the celebration that was taking place at her parent's home. It was Thanksgiving, and her whole family had gathered for the day. Holidays were wonderful times in the Sanchez family, and she knew that she would be missing most of the festivities.

"Carmen Sanchez, please report to the Director of Nursing office." The voice from the intercom startled Carmen from her thoughts. Taking one last look in the mirror, patting a few stray hairs into place, Carmen turned on her heels and hurried out of the lounge.

"Carmen," said Miss Taylor, the acting Director of Nurses, "I am going to have to ask you to float this afternoon. You will be called to areas where you will be needed. Because our staff is minimal on this holiday, we may have some places where they will need an extra hand for a short while. I hope you don't mind."

Carmen shook her head. "I don't mind, Miss Taylor. In fact, it might be exciting. I understand that the census is down on the floor where I usually work. Floating will probably make the time go quicker."

"I'm glad you are so understanding," Miss Taylor responded. "For now, I want you to report to the emergency room. They just brought in some young people who were in a car accident. You will be needed there."

Carmen left the Director of Nurses office and hurried to the emergency room. As she walked through the swinging doors, she was met with the familiar frantic buzz that accompanied a serious accident. The ambulance still stood outside the door, its lights flashing.

Two police officers leaned against a wall, comparing
notes they had taken at the scene. Some people, parents
of the injured teenagers, sat off to the side—not saying
anything, just staring straight ahead. Every now and
then, one of the mothers would dab at her eyes with a
handkerchief to wipe away a tear. Carmen could hear the
dialog of the attending physicians and nurses behind the
closed curtains. The curtains parted, and a doctor in a
blood-stained lab coat hurried to the parents. "They are
lucky kids. A few broken bones, bruises, and abrasions,
but nothing life threatening. We would like to keep them
for a day or two for observations, just to make sure, but I
am sure they are going to be just fine." One of the
fathers began to weep openly. "Thank God," he sobbed,
"thank God."

Carmen was moved by the father's emotional
expression and by his prayer of thanksgiving. "Yes," she
thought to herself, "thank God. In spite of the pain and
mending they will have to endure, the young people will
live. That was surely a gift to be thankful for."

The doctor turned and started back to the curtained
cubicle. He saw Carmen standing at the nurse's station.
"Oh Carmen," he said, "I am glad you are here. We have
everything under control, but we need someone to take
some blood samples to the lab. They are short-handed
today, too. Would you mind taking some vials over to
them?"

"Not at all," Carmen answered. "I am happy that you
do not have more to do than take care of a few bones and
cuts. It could have been worse, couldn't it?"

"It is a wonder at least one of them wasn't killed," he
said. He reached behind the curtains. "Hand me those
blood samples that have to go to the lab." He withdrew
his hand in which were four small test tubes and gave
them to Carmen. "Here you go. Thanks for running
them over for us."

Carmen turned and left the emergency room. Her errand would take her through 2 West, the floor to which she was normally assigned. "I think I'll just see how things are going," she thought. When she turned the corner that took her to the 2 West area, she encountered the family of Mr. Patterson standing outside of his room.

"Hi everybody," Carmen said in greeting. "How is your father today?"

"Oh, Carmen," answered Carol, Mr. Patterson's eldest daughter, "Dad just died."

Carmen was stunned—and embarrassed. "I'm so sorry," Carmen apologized, "I didn't know. I hope I didn't..."

"That's OK," Carol interrupted. "He passed away peacefully. Dad lived a good life. He was a wonderful father to all of us. These past years since Mom died have been hard on him. He often said that he was ready to go. He had a very strong faith. And this illness had taken its toll on him. We shall miss him. But we thank God that we had him as long as we did, that he doesn't have to suffer any more, and that he was our Dad. Thank you for asking after him. It was sweet of you to do so. You have always been so kind and good to Dad. We will never be able to thank you enough for your patience and caring." Carol reached out and embraced Carmen. "Thank you," she whispered.

Fighting back her tears, Carmen said good-bye and continued on her way to the lab. After delivering the vials, she set off to return to the emergency room. As she walked down the hall, she saw a familiar person approaching her. It was Pastor Miller. Carmen saw him often as he made his hospital visits. He always was very cheerful and treated the staff with respect. They all appreciated that, and they in turn went out of their way to see that he had everything he needed for his visits.

"Hello Carmen," he called out. "I see they have you working today too."

"Yes, Pastor, someone has to be here, and I guess I am just one of the lucky ones that was chosen. But, what brings you here today? We don't usually see many clergymen here on holidays." It was then that Carmen noticed that he was carrying the small black box that held the sacrament. "Oh, I'm sorry, Pastor, I didn't see the communion set. Someone must be very ill."

"No," he answered, "this is a strange one, the first in my experience. That is why I am so willing to be here today. Old Mrs. Morgan had serious surgery about a week ago. It was touch- and-go for a couple of days after that. But she's a fighter and she pulled through. She asked me if I would mind bringing her a thanksgiving meal today today. By that she meant Holy Communion. She made the request because this is her eucharist. 'Eucharist' means 'thanksgiving.' At first I thought she wanted to thank God for bringing her through the operation. But she is such an amazing woman. She told me, 'I want to thank God for being God; for giving us his Son so that no matter what would have happened, I still would have hope and life; and for the faith that he gives us so that, even when we are facing death, we can do so knowing that we will be well cared for.' "

"Isn't that something," Pastor Miller went on. "Thanksgiving Day is her day for thanking God for being God." He bade Carmen farewell and continued on his way.

Well, that is how Carmen's holiday went that Thanksgiving. Everywhere she turned she found thankful people: giving thanks for life, for death, for hope, for faith. And as Carmen put on her coat after her shift was over, she too gave thanks—for being able to work on this Thanksgiving Day.

It is so easy to be thankful for all of the good things in life. But, can I also thank you, Lord, for the other things that have been placed in my care: the pain that reminds me of the frailty of life; the death of a loved one that came as a release from suffering; the tasks that demand so much time and energy; the child whose rebelliousness tries my patience; the neighbor who reminds me that I should be loving and forgiving? Lord, we are to give thanks always for all things. Forgive me when I do not. Do not give up on me, but help me to see that in all things you give me the strength to endure. For that I am thankful. Amen.

The Interlude

Theme: bread of life; renewal
Scripture: John 6:14-69; Psalm 34:8
Season: 10th to 14th Sundays in Pentecost (B Cycle)

The press of traffic all the way from the city to the Villa Santa Cruz did nothing to make Paul any happier about agreeing to attend the retreat. At first he was pleased that Father Don was able to pick up the signals of his dis-ease and suggest that perhaps a weekend away from all of the pressures of his home and job would go a long way to bringing a little sanity into his insane world. It just so happened that this particular retreat for overstressed business men and women was planned, and Brother Daniel, a well-qualified retreat director, was to be the leader.

But that was then, and this was now. Of course, Paul's day did nothing to pave the way into this experience. It all began with a breakfast with Maggie and the kids that was so tense the atmosphere could have been cut with a knife. "Why is it so hard to cope with kids these days?"

he wondered. And Maggie and Paul had been doing their share of quarreling. Both wondered if the other was falling out of love, too afraid to talk about it.

If that was not enough, the office was a zoo—and he was a bear. His miserable attitude sent his secretary to the powder room in tears, a staff member threatened to quit, and his company lost a major account. As if that was not enough, there were so many interruptions that he did not get near accomplished what he had wanted to do. "Instead of going on this retreat, I would have been better off staying at the office and finishing my work," he thought as he moved along in the bumper-to-bumper traffic. "Oh well, at least I had enough sense to bring my work with me. If things get too dull, which they probably will, I can make better use of my time."

It wasn't long after the retreat began that Paul discovered that he was not unique. In fact, the only one who was really excited about being there was Brother Daniel and two others who reminded Paul of spiritual "groupies." They would have been there even if they didn't have to be. During the introductions, every other person shared lives that were lived on the edge of collapse. Paul was amazed at how similar their needs were.

Paul never had the opportunity to open his briefcase. It wasn't that they were kept all that busy. In fact, that was probably what was so therapeutic. Paul and the rest were so busy back home that they never had time to move the clutter in their lives around to make enough space for other important things. Now, in time that was not filled with activity, they not only found space but were also able to get rid of excess baggage they had been carrying around for many years.

It all started the first night at the evening meal. Everyone was quite new to one another, so the conversation tended to be businesslike, safe and

non-committal. Even the meal was not out of the
ordinary: ham, mashed potatoes, and green beans. No
one was surprised.

But during the meal, Joanne, a corporate executive
who felt like curling up and dying, said, "Would you
please pass me the bread."

Brother Daniel picked up the plate with the still warm,
homemade bread and handed it to her. "Do you know,"
he said, "that Jesus said, 'I am the bread of life.' I would
like for you to have not only this bread made with flour
and water, but the bread that our Lord offers: himself.
Just as the bread we eat nourishes our bodies, so does
Jesus, the bread of life, nourish our lives in a very special
way. Joanne, you asked for the bread. Maybe what we all
need to do during our time together is to also ask to
receive the spiritual food that Christ has to offer. I would
like to suggest that we can be a part of this process by
consciously being open to what God will teach us
through our prayers, meditation, conversation, and
devotional time. Oh yes, we can't forget that even our
fellowship together can be nourishing to us."

Brother Daniel got a lot of minds thinking at that
meal. When Paul took a bite of his well-buttered bread,
he looked up at Brother Daniel, who was watching him.
He thought about Jesus' words and how wonderful it
would be to feel as spiritually fed as eating this delicious
bread made him feel physically fed. The sharing and
eating of bread from that moment on became a very
special act. They found that even making a sandwich was
done with awed respect.

But, they were soon to learn that Brother Daniel was
not finished with them, nor was God. On Saturday
morning the whole group assembled in the chapel. They
were about to receive the eucharist when Brother Daniel
held up a host and said, "We gather to receive yet
another piece of bread. This also is the bread of life, for it
is our Lord's own body. By receiving it we enter into the

most intimate relationship with him, for he becomes a part of us as we also are a part of his body. This relationship needs to be continually affirmed and renewed. By so doing we proclaim our Lord's death and resurrection and are fed with life-giving nourishment."

Paul realized now what he missed by not going to church with his family. He was always too tired. Sunday was his only day to take it easy, but he often didn't. As he returned to his seat after receiving the host, he thought, "What a stupid oaf I have been. I have been starving myself. No wonder life has lost its meaning."

Brother Daniel had one more surprise for his group. It took place on the last day, just before departure time. Most of the people there had already changed a bit. A couple were sorry to see it end because they felt so whole and good. But a few had not learned how to surrender, so they were as tense as when they came.

They all were gathered in a cozy room with a fire burning to ward off the cool chill and comfortable chairs in which everyone was lounging. They were looking at their journals, comparing notes from when they had first arrived to now. Some shook their heads in disbelief. Paul, Joanne, and one or two others had tears in their eyes. There was a common sense that life was too precious to waste anymore.

Brother Daniel reached into a large paper bag while he said, "Before you go, I have a gift to share." He brought out and passed to each one until all had in their hands a small, round loaf of warm, aromatic bread. He continued, "We live not merely by what we call the physical world. Yes, our work is important. That helps to sustain life. That can give meaning and direction. That can also help us to feel useful and needed. But, the origin of life is more than that. It is even more than food. We have shared bread in a very special way. We have experienced Jesus as the Bread of Life; we have received him through the sacrament to form a bond between ourselves and our

savior Now, symbolized by this small loaf, I want you to
see, hold, smell, and taste that the Lord is good. The
origin of life in Christ is not born of the flesh but of the
spirit. So be fed; be full; and be whole."

Paul didn't remember much of the trip home. He
couldn't wait to share with his family his newfound life.
Oh yes, he still had his moments: the kids were still hard
to understand; he and his Maggie did not always see
eye-to-eye; and work was work. But Paul had a new
source of strength. And he had it because of an interlude
in his life during which he was invited to receive the
Bread of Life, to taste and see that the Lord is good.

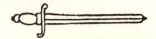

*Feed me, Lord, with the Bread of Life. Live in me and I in
you that through this indwelling your Kingdom will
come, your Will be done. In the moments of my spiritual
starvation or undernourishment, remind me that the true
bread comes from you, and that as you have fed your
people in the past, I too will be taught, strengthened,
nourished, and empowered as your servant/friend. Amen.*

The Topsy-Turvy Kingdom

Theme: the Kingdom of God
Scripture: any of the Kingdom of God passages in Matthew
Season: 8th to 10th Sundays in Pentecost (A Cycle)

Neighborhood and school bullies enjoy certain privileges—until someone takes those privileges away by exerting an influence that is more powerful and more commanding. Usually, those who are terrorized by bullies wait with eager anticipation for that day when the bullies will "get what's coming to them."

That is the way the folks in the neighborhood felt when they learned that Jason was being sent to summer camp. There was a lot of wishing going on, and it usually was, "I wish someone either straightens him out or flattens him."

But, alas, Jason wasn't at camp very long before he had established himself as the King of Section C. He had smaller and younger boys running errands for him; he threatened the bigger ones with a good thrashing if they didn't heed what he said. Jason soon gathered about himself a small band of admirers as well as a larger group who hoped there would be someone strong enough and courageous enough to stand up to him.

One of the privileges always yielded to persons like Jason is always to be first: first in line, first to pitch, first to be on the archery range, first to pick the best seat for the movie. The privilege is always announced with the words, "Me first!" After a while others don't have any hopes of being first; they are content being second or third.

One morning a softball game between sections B and C was scheduled. Jason, having the first choice because he announced that it was so, elected to play center field. He had seen the other team play and noticed they had some pretty good hitters who usually hit the ball to center field. If he played well, he would be a hero. If he didn't, he could blame one of the other players and nothing more would be said.

The teams were fairly evenly matched, and at the bottom of the fifth inning the score was tied 2-2. Both teams were playing well. However, due to a walk, a hit, and an error, section B had runners on first and third with no one out. Jason was angry, and he blamed the left fielder for not playing the hit well, even though the play should have been Jason's. The next batter was one of the other team's long-ball hitters. He timed the pitch perfectly, and the ball took off over Jason's head into the woods.

Jason went running after the ball. From the way it was hit, he knew that it had traveled fairly deep. He ran and looked, and ran some more. By this time he was really angry because he was sure the other two runs had scored and that the batter was heading for home plate. In his haste and anger, he didn't see the large root sticking up out of the ground. Jason tripped and fell.

When he looked up he saw he was near a clearing. In fact it looked like the other side of the wooded area. And, much to his surprise, he saw another camp. "That's funny," he thought, "I didn't know that there was another camp over here."

He got up and walked into the clearing. Things were a bit different over here. Jason saw that everyone was enjoying themselves. Groups of children of all ages, even some adults, were engaged in activities. Jason was suddenly aware of someone standing next to him. The realization startled him, but he tried to hide it. After all, he was tough, and this was just one more place where he would have to exert his authority.

"Hi," said the stranger. "My name is Counselor Josh. Welcome to Camp Basileia. We are about to have lunch. Won't you join us?"

"Why not," Jason answered, and he walked by Counselor Josh's side to the mess hall. A large crowd was already there, and the food line was long. Jason was not one to wait in lines, so he started to push and shove his way forward until he was near the front of the line. He thought it was strange that no one seemed to be angry or upset at him. They just smiled as he moved through the line.

But, when he was near the head of the line, someone who appeared to be the head counselor came over to him and said, "I'm sorry, but you are going to have to go to the end of the line." Jason eyed him up and decided that the counselor was too big for him to deal with. Not very pleased, he turned back, pushing as many others as hard as he could. At the end of the line, however, those who came in and took the last place were invited to go to the front of the line.

"This is crazy," Jason said to Counselor Josh. "I'm sure glad that I'm not going to this camp."

That wasn't the last of the strangeness, either. Campers who were taking seats in the back of the room were invited to the front, while Jason, who had taken a seat in the front, was asked to go to the back. When he

refused to go to the kitchen to get a pitcher of juice for
the table at which he was seated, the others just looked
at him with deep sadness in their eyes. But all of those
who were carrying food and juice to their tables were
praised and given places at the head of the tables.

Nothing made sense to Jason. No one seemed to
recognize the authority he carried with him. Other
places people would jump when he issued a command.
Here they just looked with understanding.

Finally, Jason became so frustrated that he overturned
his tray, sending plate and silverware flying. "That's it,"
he shouted. "This place is crazy. You all are crazy. I'm
getting out of here."

Jason ran through the room to the back door. He
heard shouts of warning behind him, but he was too
upset to pay any mind to what was being said. He threw
his weight against the door, which flew open and
slammed shut behind him as he thundered down the
steps. Blinded by fury he ran until the ground beneath
his feet disappeared. He pitched forward and landed with
a thud at the bottom of a pit.

The pit was not extremely deep; just deep enough to
make Jason's exit difficult. Its bottom was covered with
about an inch of water from the most recent rain. Jason
tried to jump, but the rim of the pit was beyond his
reach. The sides were slippery and afforded no handhold.
Jason, noticing a root sticking out from the side of the
pit, tried to use it to pull himself up, but it dislodged and
he was soon sitting in the muddy water. No one came as
he shouted for help.

For the first time in a long time, Jason felt afraid. He
was not accustomed to crying, but he wasn't very far
from it now. Tired from clawing at the slippery walls,
and hoarse from shouting, he sat down and said, "I'm
stuck, and I can't get out by myself."

A brief wave of vertigo overcame Jason, and when he opened his eyes he was standing outside of the pit, next to the Chief Counselor.

Jason looked into the soft, warm, compassionate eyes of his rescuer. "You know, don't you," said the Counselor, "that I couldn't do anything for you until you realized that you couldn't escape by yourself. You are so used to having things go your way—of exerting your authority, of pushing your way into prominence. Here, you see a different world. It is a world where the last are first, the servants are honored, the lost are found, and there is strength in meekness. I want you to be a part of this world, and some day you will be. For now, I hope that you will take with you your memory of Camp Basileia."

To this day, Jason does not know how he got there. All he is sure of was one minute talking to the Counselor and the next moment walking out of the woods with the softball in his hand. The three runs had scored, and his teammates, ignoring the consequences, were yelling at him. It was his fault the runs scored.

Jason looked at the angry gathering of his teammates and said—most people believe for the first time in his life—"I'm sorry."

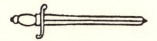

Lord, you invite us to a kingdom in which the ways of this world are turned upside down. Help me to know that in my weakest moment I am open for your indwelling. Your ways are not my ways, neither are your thoughts my thoughts. But your kingdom shall come. Amen.

A Tinker in Town

Theme: forgiveness; renewal; reconciliation
Scripture: John 3:16-17; John 20:19-29; Luke 24:13-32
Season: Passion Week; Easter (Cycles A,B,C)

There was a time, in a land long ago and far away, when there were no cities. Small towns, villages, and hamlets dotted the countryside like rows of corn neatly and uniformly growing in a field. Usually these villages were not very far apart. In fact, in a day's journey, you could visit three or four with enough time to quaff a pint or two with the locals and philosophize over the quality of the brew, which was always good.

These towns, villages, and hamlets were all part of a kingdom. But hardly anyone knew who the king was or where he lived. All they knew was that he was, and that if they needed him, he would be there. This king had no need for taxes or tribute, so the subjects of the realm rarely had any contact with him, members of his household, or even representatives of his authority.

Life was pretty much routine for the people of the land. That is not to say, however, that life was dull, nor does it suggest that their existence was without purpose.

They lived with order and under an informal kind of
hierarchy. There were persons of importance to whom
the citizens looked; they were the Burgermeisters, the
trash gatherers, and the tinkers. The Burgermeister was
important because he led all of the parades, delivered all
of the speeches, and settled most of the disputes. The
trash gatherers also occupied a high rung on the social
ladder. Under the cloak of night, these mysterious beings
would cart off whatever the people had discarded during
the day. No one knew who they were or where they took
the trash, and no one dared to stay up long enough to see
them for fear the trash gatherers would never return and
the village would be buried under a mound of trash.

And then there were the tinkers. They, above all, were
honored and respected because they did what only
tinkers could do: They mended what was broken, and
they told stories.

The people of the villages always knew when a tinker
was in town. The tinkers would walk through the streets
and sing a song, a universal song, a song that only
tinkers could sing.

Tinkerin', Tinkerin', travelin' through,
I've come to mend what's broken, 'tis true.
So give me some work, and listen you well;
I've got me a story you'll want me to tell.
Tinkerin', Tinkerin', travelin' through,
Give me some work, for my work I must do.

And so it was the tinkers would be invited to fix a
broken lock, or doll, or ax, or whisk. And while their
hands skillfully fashioned new parts for worn and
broken ones, they would tell their stories. Yes, even more
important than the Burgermeister and the trash
gatherers were the tinkers, menders of broken things
and tellers of tales.

One day a tinker came to town. He was young, and no
one remembered ever seeing him before. But he was a

tinker. He had to be. He knew the tune and the words
and he sang the song. "Tinkerin', Tinkerin' travelin'
through..." Up one street and down another he
wandered, singing the song of the tinker with a strong
and melodious voice. On and on he walked until he heard
the familiar, "Ho! Tinker!" He stopped and waited as the
cobbler emerged from the shadows of the doorway to his
shop. He carried his cobbler's bench under one arm and
the remains of a broken leg from it in his other hand.

"I've broken my bench," the old man said as he placed
it before the tinker, handing the broken leg to him as
well. "I need you to mend it," the cobbler said. "I cannot
do my work without it."

The young tinker looked thoughtfully at the broken
bench and walked around it a couple of times, surveying
it from different angles. He studied the remains of the
leg, which he held while he stroked his chin with his free
hand. Just then, out of the corner of his eye, he caught
sight of a group of children. At first it appeared that they
were playing, but upon closer examination he discovered
that they were fighting. The tinker placed the broken
piece of the leg on the inverted bench laying on the road,
and he hurried toward the children. One of them, the
biggest of them all, was bullying one of the smaller boys.
The tinker called to the children, and, instead of
running, they came to him. He spoke to them very softly,
looking with determination at the one who was
oppressing the other. In a little while, they were all
sitting on the ground, huddling close to the young man,
listening and laughing.

Well, the cobbler was not at all pleased. His bench was
not getting fixed. No self-respecting tinker would leave
his work to play and talk with children. After a while
another tinker came along and set to work repairing the
bench. He told the adults about wars that were breaking
out all over the land. Occasionally this tinker would look
up from his work and glance disapprovingly at the young

tinker, who was now teaching songs to the children. The children loved most of the songs he taught them, but they would not sing the song of the tinker when he tried to teach it to them. Their parents would not approve of that. That song belonged to the tinkers only.

Another time the young tinker was busy taking the dent out of an old pot when he saw the village idiot coming his way. Most people paid little attention to this weak-minded one. He put the pot down to go and speak with the poor creature, which made the owner of the pot very angry. She called to him and pleaded that he finish his work. The tinker held up his hand as a signal for her to be patient. That just did not do. Again another tinker came along, and when he learned of the situation he set to repairing the pot, making a mental note that when the tinkers met in the clearing in the woods, they would have to discuss this newcomer. He was creating a bad name for the rest of the tinkers, and that could not be tolerated.

The pot was repaired, which appeased the angry woman. And the village idiot found a new friend who understood him. It was a strange turn of events.

That's the way it went. The young tinker would be given a job, but something else would draw him away. One time, a couple who were on their way to the Burgermeister to draw up papers of divorce were led by the tinker to discover the power of forgiveness, which renewed their love for each other. To do this he left a farmer's horse half shod. Another time he spent some time with a young woman whom the village suspected was morally corrupt. Everyone turned away from her whenever she walked by, for fear that she would look upon them with the evil eye. But the young tinker helped her to discover a sense of worth and beauty that existed within her. This happened, however, at the expense of the carpenter whose ladder needed repairs.

The jobs were done, but always by other tinkers who came along, disapproved of the antics of the newcomer, and vowed that the situation had to be rectified. These tinkers did their jobs. They mended what was broken, and they told their tales—of sadness and misery; of hunger and poverty; of hopelessness and despair.

One night, when the moon was but a slight crescent, the tinkers gathered in the clearing in the forest. They all stood in a circle, and in the center was the young stranger. In silence they stared accusingly at him. Finally, when the owl gave its eerie call, the leader of the tinkers—the oldest and wisest—stepped in front of the young tinker and said, "You have brought disgrace upon our profession. All the time you were in the village, you never finished what you started. You always walked off and did something else. You have broken the ancient tradition of the tinkers and have defamed the song that only we sing. We accuse you of not doing things right."

Slowly the accused looked at those who surrounded him and then into the eyes of his accuser. With a firm voice he said, "True, I did not do things right. But I did do the right things." At that everyone started to shout their disapproval. "No. Don't listen to him. He can no longer be one of us. He must not sing the song any more."

The leader held up his hand for silence. "You are accused of a serious wrongdoing," he said. "You must now suffer the consequence."

The circle of tinkers closed in on the solitary figure in the middle, until he could not be seen. What they did, no one knows, but when the circle opened again and the tinkers walked away to their waiting campfires, they left the lifeless body of the young tinker laying on the hard, cold earth.

Minute followed minute, and the world was enveloped in an ominous hush. Nothing stirred. The owl ceased its calling and the moon disappeared behind dark clouds.

Suddenly there was a stirring around the clearing in the forest, and from behind the trees stepped some children, the village idiot, a couple obviously in love, the young woman of questionable character, and others whom this young man had met and touched. They moved ever so slowly toward the tinker, hoping that he would arise and go off with them. But they knew that was not to be.

They reverently circled the body of their friend, slowly knelt, and together raised the tinker and carried him off to their own secret place where he would be able to sleep the sleep of eternity without being disturbed by man or beast. Before leaving the final resting place, they promised each other to meet early every morning in the clearing in the forest to keep alive the memory of the tinker in town.

And they did. The small band of friends met every morning just as the sun began to rise. They huddled in a tight circle, drawing their cloaks and blankets around them to ward off the damp chill of the brisk morning air. They gathered; they remembered; they laughed and they cried.

One morning, a few days after the dreadful incident when the tinkers silenced the song of their friend, they were standing in their circle, arms around each other, speaking silent words of sadness and longing, when they heard, coming from the depth of the forest, a familiar voice. It was singing; it grew louder and louder. "Tinkerin', Tinkerin', travelin' through..." They couldn't believe what they heard. Some wanted to run for fear that the tinkers had found out about their meetings and might be coming to destroy them, too. But then, into the clearing stepped the young tinker. As one, they shouted for joy and ran to him, tears of joy staining the cheeks of young and old alike. They couldn't understand how this could be. But they didn't stop to wonder about it either.

What a glorious morning that was. The children played games with the tinker and sang the songs he taught them. One small girl even sang the special words, "Tinkerin', Tinkerin', travelin' through..." Their friend smiled broadly and hugged each child close and tight, kissing each of them on the top of their heads. He walked off to the side with the village idiot, and they talked of life and love and peace and joy. He embraced the young couple when they told him that a child was going to be born. The young woman blushed as she introduced the young man she was going to marry. "He thinks I'm beautiful," she whispered. The tinker looked softly at her and said, "You are. You both are. Be happy. You are worth so much."

He spent some time with everyone there. But then, as the creatures of the forest began to stir, he stood and called everyone to come close to him.

"I must leave you now," he announced.

Heads began to shake. "No," everyone started to say softly. "Don't go. Don't leave us."

"I must," the Tinker answered.

The young boy who was the bully looked into the eyes of his friend. "Where are you going?" he asked.

The tinker laughed. "Where am I going? I'm going home. My father is waiting for me to return. He sent me here to you. Now you must do for others what I did for you."

Another small child reached out and took the tinker's hand. "Who are you?" she asked.

The tinker knelt down and took her in his arms. Looking up at those who stood around him, he said, "I'm the king's son."

One more time he embraced everyone who was in the clearing in the forest, and he gave each one of them a kiss on the cheek. Finally he walked to the edge of the clearing and turned. As he waved his farewell he said, "Remember me."

None of them moved for a while. They all stood
perfectly still and listened until they could not hear the
song any more. The last they heard was, "Tinkerin',
Tinkerin', travelin' through. I've come to mend what's
broken..."

'Tis true!

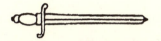

Lord, you have come and continue to come to a broken
world: a world of broken relationships, broken dreams,
broken hearts, and broken promises. You enter my broken-
ness as one who comes to mend what is broken, to repair
what I cast aside and leave for trash. As you mend
through your love and Holy Sacraments, so empower me
to be your living word that others may find wholeness and
completeness as I have found them in those you have sent
to me. Amen!

The Option

Theme: intentions, fulfilled and unfulfilled
Scripture: Romans 7:14-15
Season: 7th Sunday in Pentecost (A Cycle)

A new car has a distinctive aroma, and Margo inhaled deeply as though she was enjoying the bouquet of a vintage wine. Her right hand softly glided over the seductive texture of the velour bucket seat beside her. "I can't believe it," she whispered as her eyes scanned the instrument panel before her. "It's all mine."

Margo had waited a long time for this moment. Oh yes, she had owned other cars before. But they were all secondhand; they lasted only a short time before their repairs made it impossible for her to keep up all of the payments. But now, at long last, she had a brand-new car. And it was the super deluxe model.

She thought for a moment about how much the car cost her. Her greatest battle over the past weeks was the guilt she felt for paying so much for it. But she had saved her money for this purpose; she had put up with the inconvenience of driving other people's problems for so

long that she was able to finally feel good about her
purchase. "Besides," Margo said to the speedometer,
"this is for me, and, damn, I'm worth it."

Her hand moved quickly to her lips. She looked around
with a sense of surprise and embarrassment. Margo
usually did not talk that way. It was out of character.
She giggled nervously.

Margo knew that she did not have to buy this
particular model. But, resolved that the car she would
buy would be one that she liked, she decided to go all the
way and include all of the options that were available.
The outside rearview mirror adjusted electrically; she
could lock or unlock all of the doors from the armrest at
her left arm; there were power steering, power brakes,
and air conditioning. But there was one option that she
still felt funny about having. It was so expensive. Yet,
when she first experienced it, she was determined to
have it in her own car.

"Well, let's try it out and see if it works," she
continued as she inserted the key into the ignition and
turned it just far enough to activate the electrical system.

Even though she was expecting it, Margo jumped when
the voice spoke: "Your door is ajar. Please close your
door."

Her heart beat wildly. It was more than she had
expected. The voice was that of a male; it was deep, and
soft, and loving, and caring.

"OK handsome," Margo said, "since you put it that
way, I'll be glad to oblige you. In fact, just blow in my ear
and I'll follow you anywhere." Again Margo blushed and
giggled at her brashness. "It must be the new car," she
reasoned silently.

The sound of the voice stimulated Margo's fantasies.
She pictured a tall, sun-bronzed man with dark, wavy
hair standing in front of her. His cobalt blue eyes looked
deeply into her own. He was dressed in white slacks and
a striped pullover shirt that was open at the neck. On his

feet were white deck shoes. Behind him was a sailboat. Yes, that was it; he was holding out his hand to her to lead her to the boat. Gracefully he leaped aboard and reached down to lift her up. His strong, muscular arms encircled her waist and... *Blaaaaat!* The horn behind her startled her back to reality. Looking in the rearview mirror, she saw that she was blocking the way for another car to be pulled into the garage. The dealer who had just sold her the car was motioning her to start the engine and drive off.

Her hand trembling slightly, both from the fright and from the nervousness of driving her new car, Margo turned on the ignition switch. The car roared to life, the tachometer registering the rpm's of the powerful motor. "Please fasten your seat belt," the voice advised. Pulling the belt in front of her and snapping it into place, Margo observed, "Handsome, you are taking good care of me. I am going to have to give you a name. How about Ricardo? Ricardo and Margo—I like the way it sounds."

She moved the gear lever so that the pointer rested on "D," and she slowly accelerated. The car responded perfectly, and they were immediately wed: machine and owner.

Traffic was not too heavy, which caused Margo to give a sigh of relief. She knew she would have been a basket case if it had been rush hour because she would have had to look out for the weavers who drove from one lane to the other trying to get to the head of the pack. Her eyes quickly scanned the instruments. Everything was A-OK.

Suddenly, Margo sensed an emptiness inside. She was enjoying her drive, but she felt as though she would like to share her new possession with someone else. It is always better when you can spread the excitement to someone else.

"I think I'll drop by and see if Carla is in," Margo said as she turned off of the main drive onto a side street. "She will turn green with envy."

Just then a light, a blue light, a cobalt blue light in the center of the instrument panel started to blink on and off, and then it remained on. Margo was frightened. She didn't know what that light was for. She was about to pull the car over to the curb to find out if the owner's book had anything to say about it when the voice spoke. "I should remind you that you promised to take your mother shopping today."

Margo couldn't believe what she heard. Last night, she did in fact call her mother, and during their conversation she had promised to take her mother to the store for groceries. It was hard for her mom to get around since her father died. Her mother didn't drive, and she had to depend on the children to take her where she needed to go, or take the bus. But riding a bus with an armful of groceries is not the easiest thing to do.

"How did you know?" Margo asked before she realized that she didn't know to whom or what she was speaking.

The cobalt blue light blinked. Margo could have sworn it was really a wink.

The soft voice answered, "It doesn't matter how I know. You did say you would do it, didn't you?"

"Well, yes," she admitted, "but—. Oh, this is great. Here I am, talking to a computerized voice that thinks he's my conscience..."

The car backfired, shook, and the engine seemed like it was about to stall. The light became bright—almost angry.

"If you please, never, never refer to me as a conscience again," the voice said sternly.

Margo thought the car was going to quit in the middle of the street. "All right, all right," she hastily said, "I'm sorry. You may sound sexy, but you sure are temperamental. What's wrong with being a conscience, anyway?"

The car resumed its previous pace and purred perfectly. "I'll tell you what's wrong with a conscience. It is weak. It can be manipulated. It has no will of its own."

Margo shook her head. "Oh come on, you can't be serious. Why, a conscience is most valuable. It can keep you from getting into trouble, or at least save you from some very embarrassing situations."

"Not really," the voice countered. "How many crimes are committed as the result of a twisted conscience? How many people are addicted to some harmful substance because their conscience did not go into overdrive? How many children are born or aborted every year because they were conceived with the blessing of underactive consciences? No, the conscience is not the answer. The conscience too often is the voice of the desire of the person. And as time goes on, the conscience condones or encourages more and more strange things."

Both Margo and the voice were silent for a while. The light started to fade. Abruptly Margo said, "Well, if the conscience is so weak and malleable, what would be put in its place to prove the guidance we need?"

The light brightened again. Margo had the sense that it was smiling.

"The will," Ricardo said. "God's will."

Margo nodded. That made sense. That's the way it had always been. God's will brought order to a chaotic world, and humankind reintroduced chaos to the order through sin, twisted consciences. But it was still God's will at work making right that which was wrong.

"You're right," Margo admitted. "But will it be OK if I take mom shopping right after I show Carla the car?"

"Fair enough," the voice agreed.

"That's good, because we are here, and I was going to do it that way anyway," Margo laughed.

Just as she pulled into the driveway, Carla came running out of her garage. "Margo," she called, "wait until you see what I have. Come here quickly."

Margo was a bit crestfallen. "I have something to show you, too." She was disappointed that her friend did not acknowledge or realize she had a new car.

"Hurry. Come here," Carla insisted.

Margo entered the garage and saw a brand new car—just like the one she just bought, though a different color.

"Get in, Margo," Carla invited. "Look at how plush it is. And," she added with a childish grin, "get a load of this."

She opened her door and a voice said, "Your door is ajar. Please close the door."

The voice was different, and the light was light brown. But Margo had to work hard to keep from laughing.

Carla continued, "Isn't that just the sexiest voice you have ever heard? I call him 'Stanley' after my childhood sweetheart."

Margo nodded her head.

"Now," Carla concluded, "what is it that you wanted to show me?"

"Never mind," said Margo. "You'll find out soon enough."

The brown light blinked.

Margo winked back.

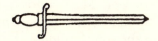

I am easily sidetracked, Lord. Even when I know what I should do, I often find other things, more pleasurable things, less burdensome, and almost always selfish. I have too many options, and that usually leads to guilt. I need your guidance. Speak to me and lead me so that, responding to your will, I will be both faithful and obedient. Amen.

Karen's Night to Polka

Theme: wholeness
Scripture: Joel 2:28-29
Season: Pentecost Sunday (A Cycle)

Karen stared out the window. She welcomed the break in the seemingly endless line of young people who came to the Office of Student Affairs for help regarding scholarships or scheduling. It was one of those days when she wished she could throw off those things that prevented her from doing what she wished with all her heart she would be free to do. Karen didn't want to be cooped up in her tiny office. She would rather be able to drive into the countryside and run through the fields, feeling the wind blow through her hair, or go out to the athletic field and play a set of tennis. But, Karen was in her office; some students were waiting to see her, and she couldn't do what she wished she would be free to do.

Her thoughts turned to that glorious Saturday in October when she and her mother traveled from their New Jersey home to a small town in Pennsylvania to be present at the wedding of her cousin. Karen liked weddings. It was a time for family reunions and celebration. This one was no exception. She remembered how beautiful Debbie was in her long, flowing, white gown and how proud her father had looked as he escorted her down the aisle. George, the groom, stood tall and handsome, hiding the nervousness he confessed to following the Service of Worship.

It was such a grand wedding. The church was full, the attendants were beautiful, and the groom's men looked smart in their rented tuxedos. Karen had felt excited when the pastor entered the pulpit to deliver the wedding homily. She had heard him preach once before, at a funeral. She remembered how helpful his words were for her at that time when she was going through her own personal crisis. Again, the pastor's meditation touched not only the bride and the groom, but everyone who had come to be a part of that worship experience.

Karen leaned back in her chair and closed her eyes. She remembered the reception following the wedding. That was the part Karen had enjoyed the most. There she had time to speak with friends and relatives she saw only on occasions such as this one. There is something special about sitting at a table with a lot of people, conversing and eating a delicious meal. At first Karen blushed when some guests, caught up in the happiness of the occasion, started to tap their forks against the water glasses—a signal that the bride and groom should kiss. But after a while, Karen's shyness left her and she started the signal a couple of times herself.

After the delicious dinner, the band took their place and the dancing began. The dancing was the most exciting part of the evening for Karen. It was the time she was able to free her spirit and allow it to soar. She thrilled at the slow dances and at the couples who held each other close, looking deeply into one another's eyes with intense love. The fast dances were exhilarating, and they left Karen almost breathless from all of the motion that blurred around her.

So the evening wore on, and Karen could not remember ever enjoying herself as much as she was that night. Then the band leader announced that they were going to play a polka. "A polka," she said out loud, clapping her hands. Of all the dances she loved the polka the best. The familiar sounds filled the banquet hall and couples filed to the dance floor. Their feet moved with almost clockwork precision, and they twirled, circled, laughed, and, yes, someone whistled. Karen laughed. Someone always whistled during a polka. Around and around they went, and Karen felt the familiar tingling in her feet as the dance went on.

Finally the dance came to an end. The dancers all but collapsed from exhaustion and the band announced an intermission. Karen caught sight of the pastor across the room. He too was dancing, and Karen especially liked the way he and his wife danced the polka. She decided that she would go to him and tell him how much she enjoyed the service and watching him dance. Slowly and laboriously, Karen got to her feet. It was difficult for Karen to walk. Her cerebral palsy had mostly affected her feet, legs, and her walking.

"Pastor," Karen said, "I just want to tell you how beautiful the wedding was today. Your sermon was very meaningful, just as it was when I came for Marc's funeral. I really enjoy listening to you. And I also enjoy watching you dance. You polka well."

Before the pastor could say anything, Karen continued, "You know, there are three things I wish I could do. I wish I could run in the fields and feel the wind blowing in my hair. I wish I could play tennis. And I wish I could dance the polka. While I was watching all of the dancers, I felt a kind of freedom, a freedom that I do not have in my legs. Even though I was sitting at the table watching, I felt as though I was out there on the dance floor. Tonight, it felt as though I was out there dancing the polka, too. That is the kind of freedom I feel that God gives me. And some day I, too, will be able to dance the polka in his Kingdom."

With that, Karen turned to return to her seat. Slowly and with difficulty she made her way back to where her family was seated at the table. As she crossed the dance floor, she once again felt the tingling in her feet, and then she knew that she would never forget the night that she danced the polka.

A knock on the door brought Karen back from her remembering. "Ah, yes," she said softly, "the students are waiting." She struggled to her feet and waited as the door opened. She smiled. "Yes," she said to herself, "I have a freedom that releases me from the limitations of my legs. Thank you, Lord."

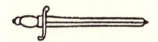

Lord, I thank you for that freedom I get from you that transcends my limitations. It is through your blessing that I am able to speak when I would be silent; act when I would be still; believe when I would doubt; rejoice when I would be in mourning; and dance in your kingdom in praise of your gracious mercy. And thank you for freeing all of your children so that, though bound by infirmity, in the spirit they can run in the fields and feel the wind blowing in their hair; play tennis; and dance the polka. Amen.

The Vacation

Theme: the meeting of the sacred and the profane
Scripture: Psalm 2:1-4
Season: Transfiguration (A Cycle)

Something was wrong. The office door, which normally was closed, stood ajar. And it was quiet. Usually the air was full of the sounds of activity. Now silence hung like an ominous pall over the complex.

Gabriel, seated behind his own desk in the outer office, glanced fearfully toward the open door. He wanted to investigate, but he was torn between the fear of what he might find and the consequences of disturbing the occupant of the inner office.

Finally Gabriel walked to the open door. He took a deep breath and looked into the still room. What he saw startled him. It was as bad as he had expected, perhaps worse. Instead of the animated industry that was his usual nature, the Lord sat behind his desk. The room was dark, the drapes closed to keep out the bright light of the day. The Lord's elbows rested on the polished top of the well-worn desk as he massaged his temples.

Gabriel broke the silence by clearing his throat and saying, "Excuse me, Lord. I didn't mean to bother you, but are you all right? I didn't hear anything, so I decided to look in."

The Lord looked up, squinted against the darkness of the room, and replied; "Oh, it's you Gabe. I'll be OK. It's just that I have this headache you wouldn't believe."

Gabriel, embarrassed at his intrusion, said, "I am sorry I disturbed you. If there is anything I can do, just let me know." He turned to leave the room.

"No, don't go," the Lord hastily said. "I guess I need someone to talk to. It's just that there is so much to do: so many prayers to deal with; so many people with problems; so much unrest; so much pain. It is getting to be almost too much for me. I am ashamed to say it, but I am tired."

Gabriel walked closer to the desk. "Lord, if you don't mind my saying so, I think you need a rest. You ought to take a vacation. When was it that you last had time for yourself?"

The Lord had to think a bit about that one. "Let me see. There was that day after creation. And there really wasn't much to do while Noah and his family were sailing around in the Ark. Then there was..." He thought but could not add anything else. "I guess that was the last time."

"That's exactly what I mean," said Gabriel. "It has been too long. No wonder you are overwhelmed. Even if a thousand years are like a day to you, you just can't keep going on. You should take some time off. You can do it. There are enough of us here who know the ropes. We can take over for a while. After all, what harm could come of things in just a short time? I've been with you now for many eons, and there is Michael, the Heavenly Hosts, and all of the Cherubim and Seraphim."

"You know, you're right, Gabriel. That's just what I am going to do. It would probably do me a world of good to get away for a bit."

The Lord came out from behind his desk and put his arm around Gabriel's shoulder as he walked him to the door. "Thank you, Gabriel. I am going to put you in charge. You can organize things. Get whomever you need to help you. I'm not going to waste any time. I think I will go somewhere I've always wanted to go."

"Where's that, Lord?" Gabriel questioned.

"Miami," came the reply.

Well, it didn't take the Lord much time to get ready, and in almost the twinkling of an eye he stood at the front desk of an oceanfront hotel where he registered under the name of Al Shaddai.

The desk clerk took the registration card. "Thank you, Mr. Shaddai. Will you be paying by cash or credit card?"

"Oops," he thought to himself. "That's one thing I didn't think of." But since he was the Lord, he could handle it. "Credit card," he answered.

"Which one?"

"Master Card, of course. What else? By the way, how much is it going to be?"

"That'll be $148 a night, plus tax."

"What?" stormed the Lord. "It's a sin to ask that much just for a place to sleep. Besides, I don't sleep."

"Sorry, but that is what it costs to use that room. If you don't want it, there will be someone along pretty soon who will pay the price."

"Oh, what's the use? I came here for a vacation. I am going to have to pay the price for it. But, it sure seems like a lot of money to pay when I am not going to be using it very much."

After the Lord settled in his overpriced room, he rented a beach umbrella and a beach chair, found himself a quiet spot, and settled down to enjoy his vacation. He was a sight to behold: a portly person, long white beard blowing in the brisk breeze, white zinc sunblock on his nose and lips, sipping on a frosted pina colada.

"Sol Libowitz from Peoria," a voice said from his right side.

"Huh? What?" the Lord said, rousing from a nap (a nap, mind you; the Lord was taking a nap!). "No, Al Shaddai from—"

"No, my name is Sol Libowitz. My wife and I just got in today. Boy, what a drive. It is not only a long way, but driving that far with my wife makes it a longer trip. Did you drive or fly?"

"I flew."

"Really? What airline?"

"I have my own transportation."

"Hey, hey! Business must be good. Wish I could say the same for myself. I had a good business going. My partner and me had Peoria all sewed up. Then came the fire. Thank God for fire insurance."

"Your welcome."

"What?"

"Sorry. It is just a habit I've gotten myself into."

"What brings you here?"

"Oh, I guess it is because of my work, too, and a flood."

"A flood! Wow! How do you start a flood?"

"What?"

"It's just a joke that people in business always tell. It's about these two businessmen who meet on the beach—"

"Never mind, I catch the drift."

The Lord closed his eyes again, trying to signal his talkative neighbor that he really didn't want to talk.

"She always wants to come to Miami."

"How's that?" the Lord said, reluctantly opening his eyes.

"She always wants to come to Miami. Me, I'd rather go to Cape Cod. Not as crowded, and certainly not as hot."

"Well, why do you come?"

"You know how it is. Are you married? No, I guess you aren't, otherwise you wouldn't be asking the question."

"Why don't you go to Cape Cod?"

"Well, she deserves it. Sarah works hard. She raised the kids real good and is a good wife. I don't spend too much time with her when I am working. And she's stuck by me when I'd given her many good reasons to leave. So I figure, why not? I can put up with Miami for a week or two if she can put up with me."

Just then a bevy of young beauties dressed in the most revealing bikinis walked in front of the two men.

"Oh God, will you look at that," Sol said.

"I am."

"What did you say?"

"Sorry." *Sure beats fig leaves,* the Lord thought to himself, knowing that that would totally confuse Sol.

The young girls met up with a group of young men who appeared to be waiting for them. They paired off and walked in differing directions.

"Ah, young love," Sol said.

"Sure is a beautiful thing to see," replied the Lord.

"Yes, it is. Sarah and I were like that one time. Now we are older. We don't look quite as good in bathing suits. I don't anyway. Sarah has kept her figure and still looks pretty good. She's a bit heavier, but all in the right places, if you know what I mean."

"Yes, I do."

Another voice could be heard. "Paging Al Shaddai. Mr. Shaddai. Phone call for Mr. Al Shaddai."

"Over here, son," the Lord answered.

The bellhop handed the phone to the Lord and waited.

The Lord looked at him, expecting him to leave. But he just stood where he was.

"I think he wants a tip," Sol said.

"Oh. OK." Looking up at the young man, he said, "Be careful of your friend Sidney. He is going to get you into trouble."

Shaking his head, the bellhop walked away as Sol laughed. "That's not the kind of tip he was expecting."

The Lord picked up the receiver. "Hello, Al here."

"Lord," Gabriel's voice said with some urgency, "I hate to interrupt your vacation, but I think you better get back here right away."

"What's wrong?"

"Well, we were doing all of the things you wanted us to do, but trouble broke out. Michael became impatient with all of the tension present in the world, so he started to gather his troops. He wants to invade the earth and put things right again. The Seraphim and Cherubim aren't speaking to one another because each one thinks the other's responsibility is more important. And I am getting a headache you wouldn't believe."

The Lord chuckled. "All right, Gabe, I'll be back soon."

"Trouble with the business?" Sol asked.

"Yes, you might say that."

"I know how it is. I never came down here that I didn't have to go back too. Sometimes I think my partner was in the wrong line when God was handing out brains."

"I'm not sure I understand. I don't do things that way."

"You know," Sol observed, "you are a nice guy, but sometimes you say the strangest things."

"Yes, I know. Others have told me the same thing. Well, I've got to go now. So long."

"Good-bye Al," Sol said, "It's been good talking to you. Will I see you again next year?"

"I don't know. Maybe. Yes, I think you will."

"Good, let's meet right here, God willing."

"I am," was the Lord's response.

It wasn't very long before the Lord was back in his office, order restored, and the kingdom humming. Gabriel knocked softly on the door.

"Come in."

"I just want to tell you that it is good having you back again."

"Thank you. It is good to be back."

"How was the vacation?"

"Great. Just great! People still know me. They talk about me pretty much. Sometimes they use my name when any other name would serve as well, but that is nothing to be worried about. And Gabriel, even though there is a lot of pain and tension, anger and vengeance, people still do love one another. I guess there is still hope. It makes all we do worthwhile."

Gabriel nodded his head. "Well what about next year? Are you going back?"

The Lord laughed. "Yes, I think I will. I have a date to meet someone on the beach. I have a feeling that we still have a lot to talk about. And I have another good reason to go back."

"What's that?"

"I didn't have the chance to finish my pina colada," the Lord said with a sheepish grin. "Not bad, not bad at all!"

(Special thanks to Dennis Christie, my partner in ministry, who, in one of our sessions of commiseration, gave birth to the idea of God taking a vacation and sitting on a beach somewhere with zinc sunblock on his lips and nose. Without his wit and active imagination, as well as his love for the Lord's Word, The Vacation would never have been created.)

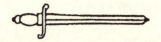

Father, can you still laugh at us when we take ourselves too seriously? Do you still have your rich sense of humor that has been so evident during the course of history? Spare us your judgment and help us to enjoy what you have given us. Help us to see you as the Lord of the dance, the God of laughter, and the Spirit of eternal joy in whom we have our hope, our help, and our salvation. Amen.

The Reader

Theme: repentance; forgiveness
Scripture: Matthew 9:1-8; Luke 7:36-50
Season: Lent; Ash Wednesday

Danny liked to read. It was a gift he had had almost from the time he could talk; and now, even though he was only eight years old, he was pretty good at it. Danny was in the second grade of school and, with his classmates, was struggling with, "Run, spot, run." Neither he nor the others did much reading out of books—only what they had to. No, Danny read people.

Danny's parents recognized this gift early in his life. At first it frightened them and they worried about how they or their son would handle this special ability. They talked about it, prayed about it, and finally realized that it was to be celebrated. So, they did not try to repress Danny's reading of people (nor did they encourage it like a cheap parlor trick). It just happened naturally, and when it did they spent time talking to Danny about it.

At first Danny's readings were just simple observations: "That lady is happy" or "He is so sad." But as time went on, the gift developed. His parents often reminisced with one another about the day they realized Danny was not only observant but that there was something deeper to it—something more full of wonder.

One day, Danny and his mother had stopped at the office where his father worked. They were shopping and were in the vicinity of the office building. "Let's surprise daddy," his mother had said. "Maybe he'll take us out for lunch."

This made Danny very happy. He liked visiting his father at work. He especially liked to sit in his big chair and spin around and around.

Well, they paid their visit, and Danny did get to sit in the chair and spin. Then his father suggested that they have lunch together.

"Oh boy," Danny had thought to himself, "a grilled cheese sandwich." His mouth watered at the thought of his favorite lunch.

As Danny sat in the big chair and waited for the grownups to take him to lunch, he looked up and saw Mr. Billman, his father's best friend, walk past the door.

"Daddy, why is Mr. Billman carrying such a heavy load?"

His father looked out at his friend. "What do you mean, Danny? He isn't carrying anything."

"Yes he is, daddy. Can't you see it? Mr. Billman has such a heavy load on his shoulders."

It was then that Danny's father realized what his son saw. Harv walked as though stooped under a burden. He was carrying a heavy load indeed. Harv's wife was terminally ill, and the medical bills were eating up their savings. Just yesterday he and Harv were talking about how afraid Harv and his wife were that that they were going to lose everything. Their insurance had run out a long time ago. Everything they had saved was almost gone. Harv was sharing how he wished there was a way to escape seeing his wife waste away. Harv had frightened him. "Would he take his own life?" Danny's dad wondered.

That day Danny had seen Harv's life burden pressing down. But that was just the beginning. His ability became keener as time went on. He was soon able to read people just by hearing about them. "I like Jesus," he said one day as they were returning home from worship. "He is so wonderful to read." Danny's parents remembered the conversation they had that day at the dinner table. They learned so much about Jesus from their little boy. That night they even thanked God for their son's gift.

Danny had been listening very carefully that Ash Wednesday when his pastor was speaking. "Jesus doesn't want his disciples to make a show of their repentance, of saying 'I'm sorry' for my sins. Instead, he wants their lives to be changed; to be different. The ashes we will receive are a sign of repentance for the sinner; not an announcement to others about how righteous we are."

Danny had leaned over to his father. "Pastor is right," he whispered. "Jesus doesn't what us to show that we are forgiven. He wants us to show our forgiveness."

When they had returned home that night, his father asked him what he meant by his observation that Jesus wants us to show our forgiveness, not that we are forgiven. "Don't we show to others our sorrow for our sins by receiving the oil and ashes?"

"Yes, we do," Danny had answered. "But that is not what Jesus wants us to announce to others."

"I don't understand," his father said.

Danny tucked his legs under him. "Don't you remember what Jesus said to people who came to him? He knew they were sinners and he forgave them. Sometimes they were sick and he healed them. But he always told them to do the same thing."

"What was that?"

"Don't you remember? He told them to sin no more. We show forgiveness by being willing to forgive others and by not sinning again."

That had been quite a night. The father of the reader of persons had tucked his son's covers in around him. He smiled at the small boy as his eyes closed and as he started to breathe the deep breaths of sleep. He had leaned down and kissed Danny on the forehead. The smudge of ashes was almost gone. How true it was! The sign is not the ashes. The sign is the love, mercy, and forgiveness of God through Jesus. And Danny's father heard the words echoing in his mind, the words of a Lord whose life was given so that others may live: "Go and sin no more."

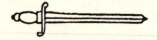

Merciful Lord, when you read my life, you discover chapter after chapter of foolish wandering, unresolved guilt, unfounded fears, sins not confessed, prayers not offered, and deeds not done. Forgive me and let me hear: "Your sins are forgiven, go and sin no more." Though long since faded and washed away, let me feel the cool tracing of the cross of ashes on my brow, and let me wear your love through my mercy, love, and forgiveness toward others. Amen.

Index

SCRIPTURE REFERENCES

Mark
    1:9-11, 52
    9:2-9, 52
    12:41-44, 47
    15:42-47, 38
Matthew
    9:1-8, 119
    17:57-61, 38
    Kingdom of God passages, 89
1 Peter 2:9-10, 23
Psalm
    2:1-4, 112
    34:8, 84
Romans
    7:14-15, 102
    10:13-15, 43

SEASONS

Advent
    3rd Sunday (B Cycle), 57
Christmas, 47
Easter
    Passion Week (Cycles A, B, C), 94
    Vigil, 38
    5th Sunday (A Cycle), 23
    6th Sunday (A Cycle), 67
Festival of St. Andrew, 43
Festival of Sts. Simon and Jude, 67
Holy Trinity (B Cycle), 28
Labor Day, 62
Lent, 74
    Ash Wednesday, 119
    1st Sunday (C Cycle), 28
    3rd Sunday (B Cycle), 16; (C Cycle), 43
Pentecost, 3
    Pentecost Sunday (A Cycle), 108
    6th Sunday (C Cycle), 78

MORE STORIES TO GROW BY!

THE MAGIC STONE and Other Stories for the Faith Journey
by James L. Henderschedt
Paperbound $7.95
95 pages, 5½" x 8½"
ISBN 0-89390-116-4

Share the word of Scripture in the context of today's lifestyles. These stories will make you want to read them aloud to let the word come to life for your congregation, prayer group, or adult education class. Readers and listeners alike are invited to think—about the "moral" of the story, about the story's significance in their lives, and about how this story can help their spiritual growth.

ANGELS TO WISH BY: A Book of Story-Prayers
by Joseph J. Juknialis
Paperbound $7.95
136 pages, 6" x 9"
ISBN 0-89390-051-6

A delight to read as a collection of stories, as well as a book well suited for use in preparing liturgies and paraliturgical celebrations. Scripture references, prayers, and activities that show how these story-prayers can be put to practical use in your parish situation accompany most of the stories.

WINTER DREAMS and Other Such Friendly Dragons
by Joseph J. Juknialis
Paperbound $7.95
87 pages, 6" x 9"
ISBN 0-89390-010-9

Allow these 15 gentle stories to take you to a world of things hoped for and to a world of things not seen. This book of dramas, fairy tales and fables dances with images that spark into clarity old and treasured principles. Discover the blessings concealed in "If Not For Our Unicorns" and "In Search Of God's Tracks."

WHEN GOD BEGAN IN THE MIDDLE
by Joseph J. Juknialis
Paperbound $7.95
101 pages, 6" x 9"
ISBN 0-89390-027-3

Here is fantasy adventure for young and old alike. In this collection of stories, find out what lies "Twixt Spring and Autumn" and "Why Water Lost Her Color". Meet Greta and Andy, whose mountain is "Carved Out of Love."

A STILLNESS WITHOUT SHADOWS
by Joseph J. Juknialis
Paperbound $7.95
75 pages, 6" x 9"
ISBN 0-89390-081-8
Enjoy this latest thought-provoking release by Joseph J. Juknialis. This collection contains 13 new stories, including: "The Cup," "The Golden Dove," "Bread that Remembers," "Golden Apples," "Pebbles at the Wall," and "Lady of the Grand." You'll find an appendix that tells you how to use the stories in church, school, or home.

NO KIDDING, GOD, WHERE ARE YOU?
Parables of Ordinary Experience
by Lou Ruoff
Paperbound $7.95
100 pages, 5½" x 8½"
ISBN 0-89390-141-5
See how Gospels come alive in today's most enthusiastic language and symbols. Gifted storyteller, Fr. Ruoff, helps finds God for those who sometimes feel that he is hiding. These 25 stories work as effective homilies and are great for your planning - they are accompanied by Scripture references according to each season of the liturgical year.

Fresh Storytelling In Ministry Ideas!

TELLING STORIES LIKE JESUS DID:
Creative Parables for Teachers
by Christelle L. Estrada
Paperbound $8.95, REVISED & EXPANDED!
100 pages, 5½" x 8½", ISBN 0-89390-097-4
Bring home the heart of Jesus' message by personalizing the parables of Luke. Each chapter includes introductory comments and questions, an easy-to-use storyline, and discussion questions for primary, secondary, and junior high grades. Newly revised.

BALLOONS! CANDY! TOYS! and Other Parables for Storytellers
by Daryl Olszewski
Paperbound $8.95
100 pages, 5½" x 8½", ISBN 0-89390-069-9
Learn how to make stories into faith experiences for children and adults. Learn to tell about "An Evening With Jesus" and "From Hostility to Hospitality". Nine delightful parables plus commentary that shows readers how to tell the stories, how to use them in preaching and teaching, and how to come up with new stories.

Stories for Children

BOOMERANG and Other Easter Stories
by Fr. Chester Wrzaszczak
Paperbound $7.95
100 pages, 5½" x 8½", ISBN 0-89390-131-8
Allow Fr.Chester's Depression-era childhood stories to entertain you ten times over. This companion volume to his *St. Francis and the Christmas Miracle* brings about a bright, new Easter outlook. These ten stories will make you understand, through a child's experience, the solemnity of Good Friday and the joy of the Resurrection.

ST. FRANCIS AND THE CHRISTMAS MIRACLE and Other Stories for Children
by Fr. Chester Wrzaszczak
Paperbound $7.95
100 pages, 5½" x 8½", ISBN 0-89390-091-5
Inviting stories for adults and children written from a time when goodwill towards others, especially during Christmas, gave many a warm and renewed faith in man. Join Fr. Chester in recalling his Depression-era childhood, when money was scarce and what people lacked in money, they made up for in love and imagination.

PARABLES FOR LITTLE PEOPLE
by Lawrence Castagnola, S.J.
Paperbound $7.95
101 pages, 5½" x 8½", ISBN 0-89390-034-6
Be forewarned. When you pick up these stories, you risk being transformed. The language of children relays the message of these 16 powerful parables. Castagnola artfully reaches children in preaching, in teaching, and in the simple pleasures of storytelling.

MORE PARABLES FOR LITTLE PEOPLE
by Lawrence Castagnola, S.J.
Paperbound $7.95
100 pages, 5½" x 8½", ISBN 0-89390-095-8
Enjoy this companion volume to *Parables for Little People*. It gives you 15 imaginative children's stories with happy, positive messages. Find seven stories concerning the Gospel themes of sharing, caring, non-violence, and women's rights. Discover still other stories that retell Gospel stories—without mentioning the names of the original characters.

Stories for Growth and Change

BREAKTHROUGH: Stories of Conversion
by Andre Papineau
Paperbound $7.95
139 pages, 5½" x 8½", ISBN 0-89390-128-8
Here is an essential resource for RCIA, Cursillo, and renewal
programs. You and your group will witness what takes place inside
Papineau's characters as they change. These stories will remind you
that change, ultimately, is a positive experience. You'll find reflections
from a psychological point of view following each section to help you
to help others deal with their personal conversions.

JESUS ON THE MEND: Healing Stories for Ordinary People
by Andre Papineau
Paperbound $7.95
150 pages, 5½" x 8½", ISBN 0-89390-140-7
You know that everybody, at some time, needs to heal or be healed.
Here are 18 Gospel-based stories that illustrate four aspects of
healing: Acknowledging the Need, Reaching Out for Help, The
Healer's Credentials, and The Healer's Therapy. Also included are
helpful reflections following each story, focusing on the process of
healing that takes place. Better understand healing, so that you, like
Jesus, can bring comfort to those who hurt.

BIBLICAL BLUES: Growing Through Set-Ups and Let-Downs
by Andre Papineau
Paperbound $7.95, NEW!
160 pages, 5½" x 8½", ISBN 0-89390-157-1
Be transformed while you are deep into your own personal recovery.
This book of biblical stories acknowleges the way people set
themselves up for a let-down to come later. Papineau consoles us
in revealing that Jesus, ever the playful one, often enters the scene to
puncture a balloon, a deflating event that somehow leads to spiritual
growth.

ORDER FORM --

Order from your local religious bookstore, or mail this form to: **Resource Publications, Inc.**
160 E. Virginia St., #290
San Jose, CA 95112
408 286-8505
FAX 408 287-8748

Qty	Title	Price	Total
___	_____	_____	_____
___	_____	_____	_____
___	_____	_____	_____
___	_____	_____	_____
___	_____	_____	_____

Subtotal _____
CA Residents Add 6¼% Sales Tax _____
*Postage and Handling _____
Total Amount Enclosed _____

☐ My check or purchase order is enclosed.
☐ Charge my: ☐Visa ☐MC Exp. date_____
Card # ____-____-____-____
Signature: _____
Name: _____
Institution: _____
Street: _____
City: _____ St ___ Zip _____
Code:TK

*Postage and Handling
$1.50 for orders under $10.00
$2.00 for orders of $10.00-$25.00
9% (max. $7.00) of order for orders over $25.00